JENNIFER HAYDEN

SPEAK

NO EVIL

JENNIFER HAYDEN

SPEAK NO EVIL

ISBN: 9798724291774

SPEAK NO EVIL
Copyright © 2021 Jennifer Anne Hayden

1

Alex instantly went lightheaded. She heard the words Jack said but her mind wasn't able to wrap itself around the reality of what they meant.

The bones were her mother's. Her mother was dead.

Her mother was…*dead*.

"Alex," Jarett stepped toward her and she backed up, still trying to grasp some shred of reality.

"I'm sorry," Jack was saying.

He continued to talk but she didn't hear a word he was saying. She finally interrupted him. "I don't understand. The bones can't be

Leona's."

Jack frowned.

"I think you'd better sit down," Jarett suggested, taking a hold of her arm. She let him lead her to the couch, allowed him to gently push her into a sitting position. She rubbed at her temples as they began to throb.

"I realize this is a shock. I know you weren't expecting to hear the news." Jack's voice was laced with sympathy. "I got confirmation a little over a week ago that the bones weren't Erica's. We moved on to Plan B at that point. Your mother did disappear the same night as Erica. They're the only two missing persons linked to this area."

"You didn't say anything." She shook her head, still in shock. "This entire time, you knew the bones weren't Erica's and you didn't say a word."

"I *couldn't* say anything. I've tried explaining to you that I can't divulge information that could compromise an ongoing investigation. I was grasping at straws once we weren't able to link the bones to Erica. Your mother was a long shot. I honestly didn't anticipate a match."

She didn't allow herself to get emotional. Not now and not in front of Jack. She kept her chin up and looked him in the eye. "Do you know what happened to her?"

He straightened. "It's not pretty. Maybe you should take a minute to digest what you've heard so far."

"My mother disappeared twenty years ago. I think I've waited long enough for answers."

"Okay," he relented reluctantly. "The medical examiner has her death listed as a homicide. There are cracks in her skull indicative of blunt force trauma. He estimates she died fairly soon after she disappeared, but that's not precise. Forensic pathology will be involved and will have to make that determination. This type of thing requires more than one set of eyes. It's not figured out overnight."

"Someone beat her to death," she deduced.

He winced, then gave her a nod. "It looks that way."

"When will you know more?" Jarett asked, leaning against the couch.

"I'm not sure exactly. A few weeks maybe. Could be sooner."

The more she thought about things, the more certain she became that Butch was responsible for yet another tragedy. "My father did this."

Jack gave her his full attention. "Did you see him get violent with your mother that night?"

"Not that particular night. But I saw him knock her around many other times. She had bruises. She was always covering them with make-up. And he was searching for her that night. When I came back from the treehouse, he caught me. He had Mimi take me inside and he went off to look for Leona. He called her a whore." She nearly choked on the words. The cruel accusation was still there in her head all these years later.

"Now that Butch is gone…" Jack gave her a helpless frown. "I don't have to tell you that complicates this a lot."

"Do you know any more about what happened to him?" she asked cautiously.

"Nothing more than I've told you already. We're going over the evidence. I'm also still questioning Gypsy Cowell. So far, she hasn't given us much. I haven't told her about your mother yet though. That may change her story."

Alex struggled to keep herself in check. For so long, she'd hated her mother — blamed Leona for walking out and leaving her behind. She'd cursed the woman more times than she could count for not giving a damn. To find out Leona had been murdered…

"You have my word, I'll keep you in the loop on this as much as I can," Jack went on. "And the offer's still on the table if you're interested in talking to Gypsy Cowell yourself. It's possible she knows more than she's letting on. There are things that don't add up with your father. She may be able to clear some of that up if you can get her to trust you."

"She's a stranger to me." Now that she knew Leona was dead, Gypsy's betrayal seemed even more heartless.

"I understand that," Jack responded equably. "I'll let you think about things. And again, I'm sorry."

She nodded halfheartedly.

He left. When she and Jarett were alone again, he took a seat next to her on the couch. "I'm sorry, Alex. I'm not sure what to say."

"I thought she left me behind." She kept her voice surprisingly even. "All these years, I thought she took off and never looked back."

He remained silent.

"I don't know why I'm surprised. I remember Butch's anger that night. He was spoiling for a fight. Mimi knew it. She made sure she had me tucked into bed before he came home."

"Was he gone all night?"

She struggled to recall. Eventually she could only shrug. "I didn't hear him come in. But he was there in the morning when I got up. That's when he started laying into me. Mimi stopped him with her shotgun. She kicked him out and

I didn't see him again until the day of her funeral."

His eyes were filled with sympathy. "Jack will figure this out. I know that's not going to relieve the pain you're feeling right now but it might make a difference down the road."

She had a hard time believing that. There was just too much happening all at one time. First Mimi, then Butch, now Leona. She'd lost her entire family, all within the span of a few weeks.

She reminded herself that she'd hated her father. Then she tried to steel herself from grieving for Leona. It was impossible to know what the woman's state of mind had been the night she'd disappeared. It was conceivable she'd been running away and Butch had caught her. There was a possibility she very well had left Alex behind intentionally.

"Don't sit here and think about every terrible scenario. That won't get you anywhere."

She scrubbed her hands over her face. "I need some answers. I can't just let this go. Even though they're both dead, I still need to know what happened."

Before Jarett could reply, his phone rang. He glanced at the caller ID and grimaced. "It's Ellery."

"You'd better take it," she advised. The way

things had been going…

He must have been thinking the same thing because he answered the call tersely. He listened for a minute. "What? When?" He listened again. "Calm down. I'll be there as soon as I can." He hung up, already getting to his feet.

"Now what?" She was almost afraid to hear.

He met her gaze, a concerned frown on his face. "Anne Marie was attacked at the vineyard. She was on her way back from the guesthouse when somebody jumped her."

She stood up abruptly, alarmed. "Attacked! By who? Is she okay?"

"She's conscious. I heard her in the background. Other than that, I don't know much." He reached for his coat. "I hate to leave you here alone. You can come with me if you want, but I need to go over there."

"You go. I'll be okay here."

He was gone a moment later. She locked up behind him and leaned back against the door wearily. Everything seemed very surreal suddenly. She felt like she was trapped in a nightmare and she had no idea how to wake herself up.

.   .   .

By the time Jarett reached Casa Bell-Rhodes, Jack was there. There were two other patrol cars parked in front of the house, as well. When Jarett walked into the foyer, he was met by Mercy, who was in the hallway, pacing.

"What the hell happened?" he asked.

"I don't know. Anne Marie was at the guesthouse talking to me. She left to go back home and the next thing I know, Ellery's calling me, hysterical. He scared the hell out of me. I thought she was dead." Close to completely unraveling, Mercy attempted to catch her breath.

"I heard her talking in the background when Ellery called me. She must be okay."

"She's lucid."

"Where is she?"

"Upstairs. Ellery called her doctor. He's up there and so is Jack."

"I'll be back in a minute." He took the stairs two at a time. The master bedroom was at the end of the hallway. The door was open. He could see Anne Marie was lying in the middle of a king-sized bed, the covers pulled up over her waist. Her face was bruised and battered. She was clearly very upset. He actually found himself feeling sorry for her.

Ellery noticed him right away. "You can come in. Doc examined her. She's bruised up.

Mild concussion. She should be okay in a day or two."

Jarett stepped into the room. He was used to hostile Anne Marie. When he looked at her and she burst into tears, he wasn't quite sure how to handle her.

Ellery sat down on the side of the bed and wrapped an arm around her. "It's okay. You're safe now."

"I really need to get a statement from her," Jack said quietly from where he stood at the foot of the bed.

"I gave you a statement," Anne Marie whimpered, swiping at the tears that were falling from her eyes. "I told you what happened. I was walking home from the guesthouse and someone attacked me."

"Did you see the person?" Jack asked.

"Just a shadow. I heard…pounding." She sniffled into a tissue. "Loud pounding. I knew the hands were gone. It was late. Nobody works past sundown around here. I went to check the noise out and that's when he came out of nowhere."

"You're sure it was a man?" Jack questioned.

"I think it was a man." Anne Marie sniffled again. "Whoever it was, the person was big."

"When you say big, how big? Like Ellery?

Like me? Jarett? Try to be as precise as you can."

She stared from man to man. Eventually she shrugged. "Probably like Jarett. Taller than Ellery."

Jarett narrowed his eyes. "I was with Alex, before you get any ideas. Jack was there, too."

"He was," Jack confirmed.

"I'm not accusing you," Anne Marie said irritably, then turned back to Jack. "I know Jarett. If it had been him, I would have recognized him."

"Was there anything familiar about the person? Maybe a scent or the sound of a voice?" Jack questioned.

She thought for a moment. "Nobody spoke to me. I don't remember any kind of scent, either." She grew agitated. "I wasn't thinking clearly and it was dark. The last thing I remember was wishing I'd brought my phone with me so I would have been able to access the flashlight. Then boom, down I went. When I came to, I was alone."

"Okay," Jack relented. "My guys are doing a thorough sweep of the grounds but I expect whoever it was is long gone. I'm going to go check in with them."

"I'll go with you," Jarett said, following.

When they reached the foyer, Mercy was still

there pacing. "Is she okay?" she asked, clearly concerned.

"She should be fine," Jarett supplied. "Are you going to stay here at the house tonight?"

She hesitated. "I wasn't planning to. But now…maybe."

"Probably not a bad idea," Jack suggested.

She nodded.

Jarett followed Jack out onto the front porch.

"So what do you think?" Jack met Jarett's gaze.

Jarett shrugged. "Somebody did a number on her. I don't have any idea who it could have been."

"You got any new hands on the property? Any new employees?"

Jarett shook his head. "Not that were hired by me. You'd have to ask Ellery. We hire separately a lot."

"What about any recent problems? I asked both Anne Marie and Ellery, but the only person they claim to have any type of issue with is Alexa Grail, besides you."

Jarett grimaced. He should have expected as much. "We already talked about me, and Alex was with us at the time Anne Marie was attacked. She's also a woman. A *small* woman."

"I'm aware of that." Jack seemed uneasy.

"I could give you a long list of people who have a problem with Ellery and Anne Marie. Let's start with the man she's been having an affair with. We can go on to the woman Ellery was sleeping with a while back. There's a good chance both of those people are married, as well. Do you want me to go on?"

Jack frowned. "I realize Anne Marie and Ellery aren't as popular as they might think. I'll be checking into those angles. But I still have to consider other options, too."

"What are you trying to say?"

"You have to admit that since Alexa Grail came back to town, everything's gone to hell in a handbasket."

"None of that has been Alex's fault. Even the fact that she came back here to Mystery Lake wasn't her fault. Her grandmother died. She had no choice but to handle the funeral, the estate."

"I'm not necessarily pointing any fingers at her, Jarett. But things here were damn peaceful until she stepped foot back in town. It would be impossible for me to overlook that."

"That's bullshit. She's here trying to do right by her grandmother. Everyone in this town has been treating her like the devil since she got here. It's not right."

"I didn't say it was." Jack backed down.

"You're the freaking sheriff in this shit town. Do your job and figure this all out!" Annoyed, Jarett turned and stalked away.

2

The misty, night air was crisp and cool as Alex made her way down the trail toward Mimi's house. She had to hurry. She knew she was in trouble. She sensed the danger around her. Something was not right. Someone was behind her. She felt a presence closing in.

Turning, she nearly tripped on some overgrown shrubbery. Catching her balance, she shoved at the brambles, desperate to get them out of her way.

"Baby girl..."

She heard the voice. Her mother's voice. She turned, peering behind her. There was nobody there. Just a dark and ominous void that seemed to go on forever.

Picking up her pace, heart thundering in her

chest, her intuition told her to run. Evil was at her heels. She had to get away.

"Baby girl..." Leona's voice seemed to echo through the meadows. It was everywhere, all around Alex. No matter which way she turned, it was there.

"Help me..."

Desperate, Alex turned in another direction. She ran as fast as she could, determined to get away from whatever danger was closing in on her.

Suddenly Butch cut her off at the path. "Damn you! Damn you for being her daughter!" He reached for Alex, his meaty fingers cutting into the skin of her arm.

Alex shut her eyes as fear clawed at her from every direction. She braced herself for whatever punishment Butch had to offer. The punishment never came...

Suddenly she was up in the treehouse. She was alone, huddled in a corner. The sound of a young girl's scream pierced its way through the darkness. Shrill, and desperate, it went on and on and on, until Alex couldn't stand it. She covered her ears with her hands and closed her eyes, willing it to stop.

Alex shot up in bed, her heart pounding a mile a minute. Her first rational thought was that she couldn't breathe. She was gasping for air and her skin was cold and clammy.

Feeling claustrophobic, she fought the covers confining her legs and eventually succeeded in kicking them to the floor.

Leaning over, she rested her hands against her knees and told herself to breathe.

A minute passed. Then another. Gradually, her world righted itself. She was back in Mimi's house, back in her bedroom.

She shivered a little, rubbing her hands up and down her chilled arms. Exhaling painfully, she got to her feet. The room felt stifling suddenly.

Crossing through hallway, she used the sink in the bathroom to splash some cold water onto her face. After drying off with a hand towel, she made her way into the living room.

She found herself shivering again. It was still warm enough inside that the furnace wasn't kicking on, but there was definitely a chill in the air.

She told herself to calm down. She'd had a nightmare. It was no wonder, after everything that had happened. She just needed to pull herself together.

She continued to tremble, her eyes scanning the living room and kitchen. She wasn't sure why, but she sensed something wasn't right. When she glanced at the door locks one by one, she saw they were all secure.

Still, she sensed danger.

She went to her bedroom and retrieved the

shotgun she'd left by the side of the bed. She walked the entire house, checking each nook and cranny for anything out of place. She found nothing.

Still, she felt no relief. Her heart was thundering inside her chest and she began to wish she hadn't told Jarett to stay at his own place the night before. It had been late when he'd called her and he'd sounded exhausted. She'd been tired herself…

The sound of pounding suddenly interrupted her thoughts. Jumpy as hell, she clasped the shotgun tightly and jerked her head toward the front door.

Thump, thump. Pause. *Thump, thump.* Pause. *Thump, thump, thump, thump, thump, thump.* Silence.

Alex felt frozen as she realized what was happening. She couldn't breathe again. Her fingers kept hold of the shotgun, but she was helpless to use it. She was paralyzed, her feet stuck to the floor where she stood.

The pounding started again. *Thump, thump.* Pause. *Thump, thump.* Pause. *Thump, thump, thump, thump, thump, thump.* Silence.

A light suddenly flashed in the window. Her gaze flew in that direction. The curtains were closed but she could easily see through the sheer material. Someone was standing there staring at her from the darkness outside. Someone with blond curls, porcelain, white skin and angry, dark eyes.

The light flashed a second time. In an instant, she was alone again. The pounding stopped and all was quiet.

. . .

Alex stared into the cup of coffee Jarett had forced into her hands a few moments earlier. She was still trembling—still felt cold to the bone. Every time she blinked, she saw that face in the window. That hair. Those eyes.

Her skin prickled again and she forced herself to breathe evenly.

"Better?" Jarett asked, sitting nearby and squeezing her neck with his fingers.

Twenty minutes earlier, she'd called him, all but hysterical. He'd obviously driven like a bat out of hell, arriving at the house within minutes. She'd barely spoken a word since he'd gotten there. She had no idea what to say. She only knew she was terrified. Of what, she had no idea. When Jarett had checked around outside, he'd found nothing. Nobody. All was calm and peaceful.

Alex continued to stare silently into her coffee mug.

"Maybe we should call Jack," he suggested,

pulling his phone from the pocket of his jeans.

"No!" She knew she sounded hysterical and she quickly lowered her voice. "There's no need. You looked around. You didn't see anyone."

He considered her for a long moment. "Tell me again what happened."

She hesitated. Then she shrugged. "I had a nightmare. I got spooked, that's all. I shouldn't have bothered you. I'm sorry."

"That's bullshit, Alex. You got me over here. The least you can do is tell me the truth."

"That *is* the truth." She forced herself to take a sip of coffee. It tasted bitter and lukewarm. She wasn't in the mood for it at all. Still, she clenched the cup in her fingers. It helped to steady her shaking hands.

"Why does it feel like I always have to pry things out of you with a crowbar? I thought we were getting past that."

She could hear the irritation in his voice and she couldn't blame him for being annoyed. She just wasn't sure how to explain herself.

"You aren't just spooked. You're scared to death. I want to know what happened here." He took the mug from her fingers and set it aside. Then he forced her to meet his gaze. "I've been honest with you about everything from the get-go. My intentions, my family, my business. *Everything.* I think you owe me at least the same courtesy."

His eyes were like magnets. She couldn't turn away from them. "It's late and I'm confused," she stammered. "This house is getting to me. After what happened to Butch, to Leona..." She bit her bottom lip. "I'm exhausted. I just freaked out a little."

"When you called me, you said someone knocked on the door. You told me someone was outside."

The sound of that cadence played inside her head again and she felt goosebumps break out on her skin. She swallowed hard.

"Alex?" he prodded.

"I heard..." She choked on the words and turned away from him. "I saw..." Her voice trailed off again. She really didn't know what to say. The more she thought about what had happened, the crazier it sounded. Rubbing a hand across her face, she leaned over, dragging air in and out of her lungs. None of it could have been real. That was all there was to it. Her imagination was playing tricks on her.

"Hey, calm down." He squeezed her shoulder, his head tipping closer to hers. "You're okay now. Everything's okay."

She let his scent wrap around her, along with the deep, gentle tone of his voice. Bit by bit, she felt her heartrate return to normal. "I don't know what I'm saying. I think it was all just a very vivid nightmare."

She felt his fingers at the nape of her neck again, subtly kneading. "You want to tell me about it?"

She thought about the dream she'd had. "I was out in the meadows. I was running from someone—Butch, I think. My mother was running from him, too. And then—" She winced at the memory. "—I was in the treehouse. I was by myself. I heard Erica screaming. It seemed so real. All of it…" She rubbed at her temples dejectedly. "When I woke up, I thought I heard knocking—that crazy cadence Anne Marie made up when we were kids. I thought I saw Erica standing there staring at me through the window. Don't tell me how crazy that sounds, I already know."

He was quiet for a long time. "I'm sorry, baby—that this is all coming back for you."

She swallowed any emotion that threatened and looked at him. "I feel like I'm losing it."

He pulled her against him, his fingers tangling in her hair. She gave into the urge to burrow against him. Instantly she felt stable again, safe. She felt warmth seep into her cold bones.

"I shouldn't have left you here alone. I'm

sorry."

"It's not your fault," she murmured against his t-shirt. They stayed that way for another minute or two before she finally backed out of his embrace. "How is Anne Marie anyway? When we talked last night, you didn't go into much detail."

"She's going to be okay. Jack's still checking into the matter. We all looked around last night. Nothing seemed out of place."

"So who attacked her?"

Concern marred his features. "I don't know. We had some trouble awhile back. Vandals. She may have caught someone in the act. There's also the fact that Anne Marie and Ellery both have their share of enemies. That goes without saying."

"What does Jack think?"

He seemed conflicted.

"What?" she asked cautiously.

"Jack doesn't know what to think," he admitted.

"Why do I feel like you're hiding something from me?"

"I'm not hiding anything." He stood abruptly. "At the risk of contributing to your coffee addiction, I could use some right now. I'm going to refresh the pot."

She stood, too. "What aren't you telling

me?"

He paused, rubbing at the muscles on the back of his neck. "Nothing, Alex. Just let it go."

She held her ground, her eyes glued to his. "I thought we were being honest here."

"Hell, you're stubborn." He shook his head irritably. "I don't think it would surprise you that Anne Marie and Ellery claim you have an issue with them."

"An issue." She frowned. Then suddenly it dawned on her. "Are you telling me that they told Jack I was the one who attacked Anne Marie?"

"No. They know you were with me at the time of the attack. But Jack's got it stuck in his craw that since you came to town everything's gone awry."

She couldn't exactly say she was shocked by the revelation. "He's right about that. But Anne Marie and Ellery are the ones who have an issue with me. Not the other way around."

"I told Jack that. He's chasing his own tail right now. He'll right himself sooner or later."

"Why doesn't that make me feel any better?" Suddenly she felt cold all over again.

He reached for her, his hands cupping her face. "I've got your back here. Don't get that look in your eyes."

"What look?"

"That look that says you're thinking about running."

She couldn't deny the idea held appeal. It would be very easy for her to call Spenser Malin and have him draw up some papers. She could sign the entire resort over to Jarett and head back to her peaceful life in Seattle with a huge sum of money. She knew her boss would hire her back. She still had her apartment…

Hell, it was tempting.

Until she thought about Leona. Someone had murdered her mother. Was her father responsible? Possibly. Until she knew for sure—until she had the answers she needed, she couldn't turn her back. She told Jarett so unequivocally.

He seemed both relieved and concerned at the same time. "You said yourself you think Butch killed your mother."

"I do think that. But I want to know what happened. I know this probably doesn't make sense to you, but I need to know whether she left me behind or not."

"It makes sense. But like I told you before, you may never get those answers."

"I realize that. I do have some things to consider. Gypsy Cowell, for one."

"I thought you didn't want to talk to her."

"I don't. But she is my mother's sister. The

more I think about that, the more I feel like I need to hear her story. Hopefully, the *real* story."

"That's probably a good idea."

She knew she needed to be completely honest with him. "I may still decide to sell when all is said and done. I can't promise you otherwise. I wish I could. I care about you—about this thing with us—far more than I want to. I didn't plan on that." It was the truth and she was glad to get it out in the open.

That got a small smile out of him. "That's something. I guess I'll have to take it for what it's worth."

3

Alex drove into town by herself later that morning. She wasn't sure if there were specific visiting hours at the jail. When she'd called Jack a few minutes earlier and informed him she was willing to talk to her aunt, he was only too happy to arrange the meeting.

She'd been a bit aloof with him. She wasn't happy about what Jarett had told her earlier that morning. If Jack had noticed her tone, he hadn't let on. He was friendly and appreciative when she walked into the sheriff's department.

The conference room she was ushered into was the same room they'd been in before. Alex knew Jack was observing the conversation through a two-way mirror that ran along one wall.

Gypsy Cowell was already in the room. She had a pack of cigarettes in front of her. She had one balanced between two fingers and was blowing out a ring of smoke from between her lips when Alex walked in.

"I didn't think you were coming."

"Neither did I." Alex slid into the chair across from her. The longer she stared at her aunt, the more she saw Leona. The resemblance really was uncanny.

"People always told us we looked like twins."

"So you said." Alex kept her voice neutral. There was no way she was letting her guard down with this woman.

"You look a little like her yourself."

"I look like Butch."

Gypsy continued to puff on her cigarette. "There you go again with the first name thing. Didn't your parents teach you any respect?"

"Not really. But then look at them. Does that really surprise you?"

Tapping an ash into a nearby dixie cup, she smirked. "You're angry as hell, aren't you, little girl?"

"My name is Alex."

Gypsy rested her elbows on the table, her eyes glued to Alex's. "Let me give you a little piece of advice, honey pie. Holding grudges doesn't fix all the wrongs in your life. Take it from someone who knows."

"From what I can see, you're a two-bit gold digger, willing to do anything for a dollar. What makes you think I'd ever take any advice from you?"

Gypsy's lips thinned into a frown. "Then why are you here?"

"Leona is dead. Someone left her bones on the front porch of my grandmother's house. I think it was Butch. Do you have any insight?"

Gypsy winced and she grumbled under her breath as she blew out some smoke. "You really are taking bitterness to an all new level."

"I'm not bitter, *Aunt Gypsy*. I'm a realist. Your actions speak louder than any words you could say to me."

Gypsy sighed. "It sounds to me like anything I say, you're going to dispute as a lie."

"Maybe. But you're my mother's sister. I can't deny that I'm curious."

"About her? Or about me?"

"For starters, her," Alex answered honestly.

"I already told you what I know about her."

"You told me why she ran away. It was a very run-of-the-mill fairy tale, with a terrible ending."

She seemed regretful. "Reality is reality,

honey pie. I'm just as upset about things as you are."

"Did my father talk to you about her?"

"If you're asking me if he confessed to killing her, no. You don't think I would be stupid enough to run off with a confessed murderer, do you?"

Alex didn't reply.

"Your father was a con. He conned me just like he was trying to con you. I didn't go searching for him, he came searching for me. I had no idea about Leona—about the fact that she'd been missing or murdered. Butch didn't give me much information about her at all."

"You must have known she was gone. Otherwise Butch wouldn't have needed you."

"He told me she left him. He didn't say when." Gypsy snuffed out her cigarette. "I told you the reason I turned him down the first time was because he didn't give me the answers I was looking for when I asked him about Leona." She popped another Camel out of the pack and lit it up. "The second time he came around—"

"I know, you were desperate. I remember what you said." Alex felt her hopes dwindling. "You must have known what his plans were once you got here to Mystery Lake. Why was he up in that treehouse? Was he planning to set it on fire? Was that all part of the sick game he was playing with me?"

Gypsy hedged.

"He's dead now. There's no money in this for you either way. The only prayer you have of avoiding jailtime depends on you telling the truth. The *entire* truth. Don't leave anything out."

Gypsy considered her options. Then she shrugged nonchalantly. "He was only trying to get your attention. He just wanted you to cut him in on what he felt he was entitled to. But when you balked and didn't take him seriously, he got angry." She paused again.

"What?" Alex prodded.

"I don't want to be considered an accessory to this crap. I had nothing to do with any laws that were broken."

"You mean besides breaking and entering at the cabin, breaking and entering at my grandmother's house and making harassing phone calls to me, impersonating my dead mother?"

Gypsy's skin paled. "I had no idea Leona was dead back then. I never would have—"

"I might be willing to drop the charges against you if you tell me everything you know. But this is your last chance. Quit wasting my time."

Gypsy arched one dark brow. "Why should I trust you?"

Alex shrugged. "You really have no reason to. I come from a long line of liars on both sides of my family."

"Well, hell…" Gypsy let out a sigh and leaned back in her chair. She looked Alex in the eye. "He got into your room at the inn. He was scavenging for information about his mother's will. He didn't find anything so he took things a step further and broke into that high falutin' attorney's office — the fat ass with the nosy wife. He got a copy of his mother's will —"

"And he found out about the codicil." Alex's stomach clenched. Clearly Butch had been smarter than she'd given him credit for.

Gypsy shrugged and nodded sheepishly. "He was pretty certain after that, that it was only a matter of time before you caved and walked away. So he decided to give you a little push."

"By tormenting me," Alex figured out, disgusted.

"He didn't put things quite that way," Gypsy defended. "He told me he was going to cause a little trouble around the campground. His plan was to make the place less appealing so you would walk."

"He dug up my mother's bones and left

them on my front porch. I tripped over them."

Gypsy inhaled and held the drag. Then she blew out a plume of smoke and cursed. "I knew nothing about that. I swear it. I wouldn't have gone along with anything so awful."

"You expect me to believe that you went along with every other crazy thing he did, but not that?"

"I wouldn't have disgraced my sister's memory that way. I would have killed the sonofabitch myself."

"I don't believe you."

"I'm not lying, honey pie. But there's nothing I can do to prove that to you. The bastard's already dead. Nobody gets to die twice."

Alex had always considered herself a decent judge of character. She was pretty good at sniffing out a liar. She wasn't getting that vibe off of Gypsy Cowell, which surprised her.

"Anything else you want to know?" Gypsy ground out another cigarette, looking a little bit hopeless herself suddenly.

"He died up in a treehouse on my property while he was trying to set it on fire. Did you know that?"

Gypsy shrugged her shoulders. "I don't know anything about a treehouse. He mentioned a boathouse. He figured that was a good thing to burn because it was near water and there wouldn't be a lot of damage to the rest of the resort."

Confused, Alex considered that. "Why would he care how much of the land he destroyed? The more destruction, the less likely I would have been to stay."

"Well, honey pie, he figured it wasn't smart to destroy the entire place before he even got a piece of his inheritance. A burned out piece of rubble isn't worth a damn, now is it?"

Alex stared at the woman skeptically, not sure whether to believe her or not.

"You asked for the truth. That's what I've given you. It's your turn. You keep up your end of our bargain and get me out of this joint."

Alex got to her feet, still confused. She met Jack in the hallway.

His expression was unreadable. His cop face was firmly in place. "You got more out of her than I did," he admitted.

"Let her go. I don't want to press charges."

He seemed surprised. "You were serious about that?"

"I gave her my word. Some people consider that sacred."

He folded his arms over his chest. "It's your call. But if I were you—"

"You're not," she said, cutting him off.

"Why was he up in that treehouse?" She spoke the words that had been on her mind for a while now.

He stared at her dumbly. "I'm not following you."

"Butch. Why was he up there? If he was setting it on fire, why would he be up inside? He very easily could have started the fire from the ground. Those trees would have lit up like a match. He would have been able to get away easily."

He frowned silently and she could tell he had something on his mind.

"What?" she finally asked, growing frustrated.

"I'm in the middle of an investigation. I can't discuss certain things with you." His voice sounded colder than usual and she took notice.

She thought again about what Jarett had told her that morning. "You think I'm somehow responsible for all this, don't you?"

"I didn't say that."

"Yes, you did. Jarett told me what you said to him last night. You think this all came about the minute I arrived back in town."

This time he winced. "I'm a lawman. I see things in black and white. I have to consider every option."

She tried not to let the words hurt. Knowing law enforcement had her in their crosshairs made her feel very unsettled. It was as if history was repeating itself, only now her parents weren't the ones under fire. She was.

Forcing her chin into the air, she made sure she looked him in the eye. "You can think what you want. There's nothing I can do to stop you. But I won't be going away. You don't scare me and neither does anyone else in this town. I will find out what happened to my mother." With that, she turned around with as much dignity as she could muster and walked away.

4

Mercy stood at the front window and stared out into the darkness. It was nearly midnight. This was the second night in a row she'd spent in the main house. Evie was bunked safely in with Clarissa. Both girls were terrified to go anywhere alone after what had happened to Anne Marie.

Ellery had hired private security that morning. He'd had more lighting installed around the vineyard. He'd insisted what happened would never happen again.

Mercy just kept thinking back to the threatening letter she'd received. She'd reminded the sheriff. She'd reminded Ellery. Neither of them had given the letter much thought. They were both adamant to blame Butch Grail for that. And Butch Grail was now dead.

She moved away from the window, a little nauseated. She was about to head to the guestroom when she heard her phone ping. She had a message from Anne Marie. Her cousin hadn't spoken to her at all since the attack so she read the message quickly, hoping everything was okay.

Meet me in your room. ASAP.

She frowned and headed for the stairs. When she reached the guestroom, she found Anne Marie sitting silently on the bed, a silk robe wrapped around her.

Mercy winced when she got a look at the bruises on Anne Marie's face. An expletive slipped out before she could stop it.

Anne Marie let out a tired sigh. "Thanks. I needed that."

"Sorry. I didn't expect—" She cut herself off. "Never mind. What are you doing in here? You're supposed to be in bed. Do you need me to get you something? Water, food?"

"I just need you to sit down and listen to me. I don't have much time. If Ellery wakes up and realizes I'm gone, he'll freak out. He's been hovering over me like a mother hen."

"What do you expect after what happened?

He could act like he doesn't care. Would you prefer that?"

"Forget about him!" Anne Marie hissed. "Sit down and pay attention!"

Mercy saw the anxiety in Anne Marie's face. She took it seriously and sat down in a chair near the bed.

"What happened last night was no random thing."

"What? How do you know?" Mercy felt her skin grow hot.

"When I was walking back to the house, I heard something. Pounding."

"Yes, I know. Ellery mentioned that last night."

"The cadence, Mercy. Someone was pounding out *the cadence*."

Mercy's lungs immediately stopped working. She just stared at her friend dumbly.

"Did you hear what I said?" Anne Marie reached out and grasped Mercy by the shoulders, giving her a good shake.

Mercy snapped out of her trance, shoving Anne Marie's hands aside. "Stop it! You're crazy!"

"I'm not crazy. I heard it. Do you really think I'd make a thing like this up?"

Mercy stood up, suddenly unable to sit still. "How could you possibly remember what that cadence sounded like? Your mind was playing tricks on you."

"It wasn't. I can do the cadence right now if you want me to. It's something I'll never forget. I'm pretty sure you haven't forgotten it, either." Anne Marie shot her a look.

Mercy refused to accept what she was hearing. "It was dark and late and you'd been drinking. Who knows what you really heard?"

"I had one glass of wine! It wasn't even a full glass!" Anne Marie sighed and took a calming breath. "You can believe me or not but I'm telling you what I heard."

Mercy felt lightheaded and sat back down again. "Who? Who would do something like that? Who else even knows that cadence?"

"We've been over this already. Alex and CeCe." Anne Marie lifted one shoulder. "I told you the other day that I thought something was off about both of them."

"You've been saying that for twenty years," Mercy snapped irritably. "And Alex was with Jarett last night. Jack verified that."

"CeCe wasn't."

"CeCe is a woman. You said you thought a man attacked you."

"I said someone *big*. CeCe is a tall woman. She's definitely bigger than I am."

CeCe Britton had never impressed Mercy as

the violent type. She told Anne Marie so.

"There is nobody else!" Anne Marie seemed to lose it. "Don't you get that? Nobody else knew that cadence!"

Mercy's skin pebbled. "What do you want me to say?"

"I don't know." Anne Marie got to her feet. She walked over and lifted the curtain back, her eyes scanning the vineyard below. "Butch Grail is dead. If he was responsible for those letters, for that phone reappearing, the threat would be gone."

"You forgot about the bones," Mercy reminded her solemnly. "Now that we know they belonged to Leona Grail, that proves Butch was responsible for putting them on Alex's porch."

"Does it?" Anne Marie's eyes looked a little haunted.

Mercy found herself shivering. "If anyone killed Leona Grail it was her abusive husband. That's a given."

"Maybe." Anne Marie wrapped her arms around her middle. "It's possible that the bones and the threats are unrelated. Leona Grail's murder would have nothing to do with the cadence — with Erica or the treehouse."

Now it was Mercy who took pause and thought.

"We're not going to figure any of this out tonight. But I needed you to know what I heard." Anne Marie sat down next to Mercy again, her expression grave. "You can't tell Ellery about any of this. He doesn't know about the cadence. Neither does Jack."

"Why not?" Mercy asked incredulously.

"They would both think I'm crazy. Hell, you did, too, for a minute there."

Mercy's silence must have set Anne Marie's teeth on edge because she swore and got to her feet. "You can think what you want. But if you're smart, you'll be very careful what you're doing. You got a threatening letter. You're part of this mess, too. We need to watch out for each other — watch out for the kids."

"That goes without saying," Mercy eventually agreed.

"I need to get back to bed. We'll talk more in the morning. Just remember, don't mention this to Ellery — or to anyone else."

"Who am I going to tell?" Mercy asked uneasily. She watched as her cousin left the room, shutting the door quietly behind her. Then she got up and moved to the window where Anne Marie had stood only a few minutes earlier. She peered out into the darkness.

The lights Ellery had installed were

strategically placed sporadically around the vineyard. She could see the glittering water of the swimming pool below, the patio furniture nearby. There was a grassy area just beyond the pool deck that stretched out a ways and disappeared into the darkness on the outskirts of the property.

She was just about to turn away when her eyes caught movement off in the distance. She squinted, trying her hardest to bring what was moving into focus. It was a person, she realized. A person who was walking straight toward the house with purpose.

Mercy's mouth went dry. She couldn't move. She wanted to scream. She wanted to call for Anne Marie, for Ellery—hell, for anyone! But she just stood there frozen instead. Her eyes became fixated on the small, blond figure as it came to a stop just under one of the security lights.

Dear God, no! Mercy thought to herself. There was no way that what she was seeing was real. She shut her eyes and counted to ten, telling herself she was imagining things. Just like Anne Marie, she was losing her mind.

When she opened her eyes and focused again, there was nothing there. The figure was gone, as though it had never been there in the first place.

5

Jarett cleared the dinner dishes from the table and carried them over to the sink. Alex was still sitting at the nook, swirling the wine in her glass. It had taken some doing, but he'd eventually convinced her to come back to his place on the vineyard. He felt better being able to keep an eye on things, after what had happened to Anne Marie.

Since her visit to the sheriff's department, Alex had been quiet. Reserved. She hadn't made any effort to talk about the conversation she'd shared with her aunt. He hadn't pushed, but he was curious as hell. He could tell something was bothering her.

Earlier, she'd spent an hour on his computer,

picking out a casket for her father. The chore had been demoralizing and he'd sensed her discomfort. Eventually she'd told the mortuary to provide whatever cheap casket was available. Butch would be buried in the local cemetery. No marker. Jarett figured that was the best course of action. Nobody around these parts would ever visit the grave. Nobody would appreciate its presence, either.

Once he finished loading the dishwasher, he walked over and took a seat next to her. She didn't acknowledge him for a full two minutes. Finally he cleared his throat.

She lifted her head, met his gaze. The exhaustion she felt was there in her eyes and he instantly felt bad. "You should go to bed."

She lifted her wineglass, took a small sip. "I'm not tired. I'll just lie there and stare at the ceiling. But don't let me stop you. I know you're probably beat."

"I'm fine." He folded his arms and rested them on the counter. "I don't want to push you, so feel free to tell me to mind my own business, but if you want to talk about anything, I'm here."

"I know you are." She leaned back and stared up at the ceiling. "I just don't know what to think anymore."

"About your aunt?"

She blew out a breath. "It's weird to hear her called that."

"I'm sure it is."

She kept her fingers wrapped around her glass. "She's odd—nothing like my mother was." She paused. "Or maybe she's just like my mother was. I can't decide."

"You don't know her very well."

"No, I don't. They look so much alike. And at times..." She sat up straight again. "At times, she sounds like Leona. But she has this drawl. It's southern. I don't know where she's from. That reminds me that I really don't know where my mother is from, either. Everything she told me was a lie."

"I'm sure your aunt will tell you if you ask."

"Maybe. I didn't care enough to this afternoon."

"So go see her again," he figured, shrugging his shoulders.

"I can't. I had Jack turn her loose."

"Why would you do a thing like that after what she did?"

She set her wineglass aside. "I guess because I asked her questions and she gave me answers. I believe those answers. I honestly think Butch conned her. Hell, *con* was his middle name." She snorted. "He really went to a lot of trouble to get his hands on Mimi's money."

He listened while she shared the majority of the conversation she'd had with her aunt. When she was done, he wasn't sure quite what to say.

"That's how I felt." She gave him a knowing look. "It's pretty crazy."

"So what did Jack think about everything?"

Her smile faded.

"Uh oh. What happened?"

"He doesn't trust me. And I don't trust him."

He thought his next words over carefully. "He's a good cop, Alex. I know I've said that to you before. This is a complicated situation. He's just making sure he covers all the bases."

"I'm not responsible for anything that's happened. I know he knows that, yet he's evasive with me. He keeps that damn cop face firmly in place all the time. The fact that he didn't tell me about my mother the minute he suspected the bones might be hers…" Her jaw clenched angrily. "It just makes me so mad."

"He didn't suspect anything that you couldn't have thought about on your own. Leona was a missing person, just like Erica Haynes. It was a natural step to take on his part. If it hadn't panned out, you would have been pissed at him for ever bringing your mother's name into things."

"Maybe so," she replied noncommittally. She got up from the table and carried her wineglass over to the sink. After she washed it out, she set it on the drainboard. Then she leaned against the counter. "I keep thinking about Butch. About what happened to him."

He turned, stretching his legs out in front of him and crossing them at the ankles. "You mean about the fire?"

"I mean about him being up in that treehouse when the fire started. It just doesn't make sense to me."

"He was trying to burn the thing down, Alex. You just told me yourself that he intended to torch the boathouse. That's what your aunt told you, right?"

"She told me the boathouse was his original target. I'm assuming he found the structure was already gone and got angry. He had to find a different place. But the treehouse?" She tapped her fingers impatiently against the granite. "That area is dry as a bone this time of year. He had to know that he didn't need to go up inside. He could have set the fire below with very little effort. It would have been easier and safer for him—no risk of getting himself caught up there."

"Who knows what he was thinking?"

Still not convinced, she kept on. "Gypsy told

me he didn't want to cause much damage. He wanted to keep his inheritance intact. In other words, burned out rubble isn't worth as much—those were her words, not mine."

"Anger does strange things to a person. Maybe he just got pissed off and started lighting matches. Maybe he didn't think at all at first. That wouldn't be so unlike Butch, would it?"

"I guess not," she relented.

He could see the stress still there in her eyes. She was obviously on the fence. Figuring there wasn't much he could do about that, he gave up on trying to convince her. He got up and closed the distance between them. He set his hands on her waist, pulling her toward him as he rubbed his nose lightly against hers. "We can go upstairs anyway. We don't have to go to sleep."

She smiled halfway. "Really. And just what would we do besides sleep?"

He dropped his head another inch, his mouth covering hers. He deepened the kiss immediately. She kissed him back just as urgently. He lifted her, setting her gently on top of the granite. "Or we could just stay right here." He flicked at the button to her jeans, popping it open.

She lifted, giving him better access. Just as

he got her zipper down, the front doorbell rang, startling them both.

Cursing, he kept his hand where it was. "Ignore it. They'll go away."

"It might be important. After all the weird things happening around here..."

The knocking on the door continued.

Giving up, he stepped back, allowing her to right her clothing. He went into the foyer and opened the door. He was surprised to find Jack on the stoop. He wasn't alone. A woman stood next to him. She was wearing a dark colored leather jacket and the tightest pair of jeans Jarett had ever seen.

. . .

Alex stared curiously from behind Jarett. She wasn't sure what to think of the scene. Jack was standing on the porch. He was dressed in street clothes—jeans and a t-shirt. He had a gun strapped to his hip. Other than that, he looked more like a citizen than he did a sheriff.

At his side was Gypsy Cowell. She was chomping on a stick of gum again—or maybe more than one stick. The cracking noise she seemed to love making instantly began to echo in Alex's head like a firework.

"I thought you might be here—" Jack began.

"He tried to arrest me again!" Gypsy exclaimed, interrupting him. "It's a mystery to me how any lawman can have so little to do that he has this much time to harass an innocent citizen."

Alex met Jack's perturbed gaze. "What's she talking about? And why have you brought her here?"

"She was prowling out at your house," he explained. "One of my patrolmen called me."

Alex wasn't sure she wanted to hear any more. She'd already dealt with enough for one day.

"I was looking for you, honey pie."

"Will you please stop calling me that," Alex said automatically. "I told you to let her go." She turned to Jack again.

"I *did* let her go. Like I said, she was prowling around your house." He gave her an *I told you so* look.

She turned back to Gypsy, the beginnings of regret starting to set in. "If you're free, why would you be lurking around my house? That's what got you into trouble in the first place."

"That was before we knew each other," Gypsy explained innocently. As if only noticing Jarett for the first time, she smiled widely. "Now who's this hunky, young man?"

Alex didn't give Jarett a chance to answer. "When I told Sheriff Frasier to let you go, I figured you would actually *go*. As in *leave town*. Go back where you came from. Hit the road..." Her voice trailed off when she saw the blank expression on Gypsy's face. The woman truly wasn't getting it. "You need to go home before you end up back in jail."

"I haven't broken any laws. It's not illegal to knock on someone's door." She gave Jack a glare. "I don't appreciate his gruff manor, either. A little charm school would go a long way."

Jack gave Alex a dry stare. She could see he was close to losing his patience. "What do you want me to do with her? Book her for trespassing—*again*?"

"I don't want to go back to jail! I just need a place to stay for the night. It's late. I didn't get released from that godforsaken dump until almost five-thirty. By then, where could I go? I can't get a cab into Morton. I can't catch a bus this time of night. Do you want me to sleep on a street corner?"

It was on the tip of Alex's tongue to say yes.

Jarett beat her to the punch. "I have a spare room. You can stay here for the night."

Alex elbowed him the ribs, eliciting an oof from him. He gave her a helpless shrug in return.

"She's not staying here." Alex lowered her voice but she knew both Jack and Gypsy could still hear her.

"She's your aunt."

"I hardly know her. She's a thief. She'll probably steal all your silver."

"I am not a thief!" Gypsy said indignantly. "I've never stolen a thing in my life!"

"You broke into my grandmother's house," Alex reminded her incredulously.

Gypsy frowned. "Butch did that—with a *key*. I didn't *steal* anything. I'll have you know that my mama raised me right. I work for what I have."

"Even for somebody else's inheritance?" Alex challenged.

Jarett pinched the bridge of his nose. Then he met Alex's gaze. "Have her stay at the resort for the night. I'll give her a ride to the bus station in the morning and she can head back to…" He glanced at Gypsy pointedly, waiting for her to fill in the blank.

"I'm not staying in that creepy, old house by myself," she said, ignoring his inquiry. "No way. I got a very bad vibe when I was in there the last time."

"Maybe that's because you were a burglar!" Alex shot back, losing her patience. "This is ridiculous!"

"I told you to leave her in jail," Jack said.

Jarett finally lost his patience. "You can stay here. I have a guestroom. I don't have any silver," he added, giving Alex a look. "All my valuables are in a safe, locked up in my bedroom. Good luck trying to get at them. I have a very nice revolver that sleeps right next to my bed and I'm a very light sleeper."

Gypsy seemed insulted. "I told you, I don't steal."

"I'm leaving," Jack announced, stepping off the porch and heading for his cruiser.

Alex scowled at her aunt.

Gypsy just gave her another blank stare. "I don't understand why you're so upset. We're just starting to get to know each other. Would it be so awful if you had me around for another twenty-four hours?"

Alex checked her watch and grimaced. "*Eight. Eight* hours. You're going to the bus station first thing in the morning."

Clearly a little hurt, Gypsy frowned. "So much for familial hospitality."

Alex was about to lose her cool when Jarett took over. "Come inside. I'll show you your room."

Gypsy's frown bent into a smile. "Thank you, honey pie."

"Don't call him that, either," Alex snapped.

Gypsy's smile remained intact as she followed Jarett into the house.

Thirty minutes later, Alex lay in bed, staring up at the ceiling. She knew she wasn't going to sleep a wink now. Not with Gypsy in the house.

"She's not going to rob me blind, Alex. There's nothing worth stealing that she can lift."

She turned in the darkness and peered over at him. He was lying on his side, his head resting on his hand as he watched her. "I don't care. I don't want her here."

"I realize that. But aside from letting her sleep on the street, what could I do?"

"Exactly what you just said. She'd have figured something out. People like her always find a way out of messes like this."

"If I thought she was a threat, I wouldn't have let her in my house."

"I don't owe her anything. I don't care if she's my mother's sister. I don't want her hanging around, causing me problems."

"I get that."

"Do you? She's a manipulator. You see that, right?"

"I see it."

"So why the hell did you let her in here?" She rolled over and glared into his eyes.

"Because she's the only family you have left and I think maybe you'll find you have more questions for her once you get past all this other BS and can think rationally."

She opened her mouth to speak, then shut it again.

"Are you okay?" he asked quietly.

"I haven't had a relative yet besides Mimi who's ended up being worth a lick of spit."

"I know it. And I'm sorry about that. But Gypsy has parents. They're your mother's parents. *Your grandparents*. Maybe someday you'll want to know them."

"I get the feeling they weren't happy to hear I was on the way." That fact rankled on her nerves and she told herself not to get emotional about it.

"That's all stuff you may want to figure out. I just put the option in your hands. I'll get her out of here in the morning if that's what you want."

"It is," she said firmly.

"Okay, baby. Settle down."

"You really don't have any silver?"

He snorted at that. "I'm not the family silver type. Anne Marie's got all that crap in the main house." He reached for her. "Now can we get back to what we were doing before we were so rudely interrupted?"

Relaxing, she slid into his embrace. His hands moved under her nightshirt, sliding up to cup her breasts. Her eyes shut and she lost herself in the sensations.

He had her shirt up and over her head in an instant. His lips moved from her breasts, down her stomach and over her navel. She held her breath when he dropped further south, finding her intimately.

Moaning, she arched her back, knowing she was close to flying over the edge. She tried to hold on, tried to enjoy the sensations, but they were too much. Her body exploded all at once. She rode the climax out shamelessly.

When he lifted his head, he had a satisfied smile on his face. "More?"

She reached for him then. He moved up and over her, resting himself gently between her legs. He slid inside her an instant later and they both let out groans of satisfaction. He dropped his forehead against hers and they began to move in unison. She told herself to hold out as long as she could, but her body had other ideas. The minute his lips found a distended nipple and latched on, she came undone for the second time, wrapping her legs tightly around him and bringing him to a shattering climax of his own.

They lay there for a few minutes, sweaty and replete. Eventually he lifted his head and looked her in the eyes. "I think you should know I'm all in here. This is the real deal for me."

Caught off guard, she wasn't sure what to say. She just stared at him silently.

"I get it. You don't have to say anything. Not yet. I'm a patient guy." He disengaged himself and rolled over, taking her with him.

A few minutes later, she heard his breathing slow into a steady rhythm. He was asleep, his arm still holding her tightly against his side.

She waited for the panic to set in. She waited for the anxiety. She waited for...*something*. Nothing happened. A few minutes later, she relaxed and rested her head against his shoulder. Before she could stop it, her eyes fluttered closed and she drifted off to sleep.

6

When Alex woke up the next morning, she was alone in bed. The sun was up and billowing through the blinds across the room.

Stretching, she lay there for a moment, enjoying the blessed peace. She knew the minute she got out of bed she was going to have to face reality. And right now, that reality was almost more than she could take.

Gathering her courage, she kicked the covers back and dragged herself into the bathroom. She managed a shower and then brushed her teeth. By the time she got to her makeup, she considered skipping the whole thing and crawling back into bed. She felt exhausted, both mentally and physically.

Knowing there was no avoiding what

awaited her downstairs, she finished getting ready and left the bedroom. When she got to the landing, she could hear voices coming from the first floor. She heard Jarett laugh. Then she heard Gypsy's southern drawl.

She thought about what Jarett had said the night before. Would she want a relationship with her mother's family at some point?

She didn't right now, she knew that for sure. She was grappling with enough and Gypsy's intrusion was just another distraction in an already complicated situation.

Biting the bullet, she went downstairs and entered the kitchen. She found Jarett leaning against the kitchen counter, a cup of coffee in one hand. He was freshly showered and dressed for the day in his usual jeans and t-shirt. His dark hair was still damp. She took a moment to appreciate the sight. Instantly she recalled his proclamation. He was *all in.*

A lump formed in her throat.

"Hey," he said, grinning when he saw her. "I thought you could use a little extra sleep." He grabbed a mug from the counter and filled it for her. Then he dropped a kiss on the top of her head as he handed it over.

"This one's a keeper, honey pie," Gypsy said from her spot at the breakfast bar.

Alex grimaced and turned her way.

This morning, her aunt was wearing a bright, red t-shirt that hugged her curves in all the right places. Her jeans were black and just as painted on as the ones she'd worn the day before. She'd clearly taken advantage of the bathroom facilities. Her hair and makeup were freshly done and she appeared relaxed. Frankly, it was hard to believe she was nearly fifty years old.

Alex grumbled a response under her breath and sipped her coffee. She'd been thinking about how to handle Gypsy's situation all morning and she hadn't come up with a solution other than the woman had to go. *Soon*.

"You're not a morning person," Gypsy figured out, arching a brow. "Most of your kin are morning people. Well, I guess your mama really wasn't. She slept like a teenager."

Alex remembered that about Leona. She'd always been the last one up.

"There are eggs on the stove," Jarett informed her when the silence went on to the point where things got uncomfortable. "There's toast, too. I need to head over to the office. I've got some work this morning. Then I'll come back and give Gypsy a ride to the bus station."

"It's fine," Alex decided aloud. "I can do it."

He seemed surprised. "You sure?"

"She's my responsibility, not yours."

"Well, thanks. I feel the love," Gypsy said sarcastically.

Jarett walked over and gave Alex a quick kiss. Then he arched a brow. "Be nice," he said, for her ears only.

She didn't reply.

Once she and Gypsy were alone, an awkward silence ensued again.

"Listen, I understand you're upset with me. I don't blame you. But I think you and I can help each other if we allow it."

Bracing a hip against the counter, Alex thought about that. "And just how would you be able to help me?"

"Well, for starters Jarett told me you're trying to rebuild your grandmother's business at the resort. That sounds like quite the endeavor. I used to work in a hotel back in Biloxi."

So that was where the drawl came from. Alex thought about that as she enjoyed her coffee. If her mother had grown up in Biloxi, just how in the hell had she come across Butch? He'd grown up in Washington on the resort as far as Alex knew. And what had happened to Leona's accent? Alex had never noticed her having one.

"You'd like Biloxi. My parents are still there. They're retired."

Knowing that curiosity killed the cat, Alex found herself diving in anyway. "What did they do?"

"For a living?" Gypsy perked up, apparently happy that Alex wasn't just hauling her straight to the car and off to the bus station. "My mother taught school for a time. My father was a banker."

It wasn't a lot of information but it seemed like a lot considering what she'd known about her mother's family before. "How did my mother end up with Butch if she lived in Biloxi? He grew up here."

"That's a bit of a story, honey pie. Are you sure you have time to listen to it?"

"If you'll stop calling me honey pie, I might consider the idea."

"I call *everyone* honey pie."

"I noticed."

Gypsy, unfazed, shrugged her shoulders. "Well, my parents traveled with us a lot when we were young. Believe it or not, we came here to Washington. We stayed at your grandma's resort. That's how your parents met. I think I was around twelve. Your mama was just about to turn sixteen."

Alex sat down at the breakfast bar. "She was young."

Gypsy nodded. "Do you mind if I help

myself to more creamer? Your hunky boyfriend there said it was fine, but I don't want to step on your toes now that we're finally getting along so well."

Alex bit her tongue. "Go ahead."

Gypsy got up, retrieved a fresh cup of coffee and added a healthy dollop of creamer. Then she sat down again. "Getting back to your mother, yes, she was young. Anyway, she and your daddy were drawn to each other like flies on—" She stopped herself. "Well, you get what I mean."

"I get it." Alex had never heard the story of how her parents had met. Neither of them had bothered to tell her. Even Mimi hadn't relayed the tale.

"After that, Leona came back here to visit at least a couple of times. Like I told you before, when she was seventeen, she got pregnant." Gypsy lifted her coffee cup and took a sip. "Back in those days, your daddy wasn't so bad. He was attractive and he seemed to dote on her. She loved him."

"I never knew either one of them when they were in love," Alex replied thoughtfully.

"So you said. I'm sorry to hear that." Gypsy rested her head on her hand. "Sometimes people change. Lord only knows why. Could be their genes. Could be they just get cussed and ornery. Maybe something happened in the marriage that turned Butch into what he became—not that I'm saying it's your mama's fault he beat her. There's no excuse for that."

"No, there isn't," Alex agreed.

"You and I aren't so different, honey—" This time she caught herself. "—*Alex*. We really aren't. My childhood wasn't any kind of comedy sitcom, either. When my sister left, everything fell apart. My parents stayed together but they blamed each other for what Leona had done. I scraped by and got out of high school by the skin of my teeth. Then I met and married my first husband." She snorted. "Real winner. Rodeo guy. We traveled a lot. That was fun. Eventually he got tired of me and I got tired of him."

"How many husbands have you had?" Alex spoke before she realized how rude she sounded. "Sorry," she added sheepishly. "That came out sounding—"

Gypsy waved a hand in the air. "I don't offend easily. I've had three. The last one was and *is* literally *the last one*. Inevitably, men cheat. They're never happy with just one woman." She lifted a brow. "Except maybe yours. I think he might be the real deal."

Alex's face suddenly felt hot. "You don't even know him."

"Oh honey pie, I can tell a good man when I see one. I just don't manage to snag that type for myself. A guy like yours would never gravitate toward a woman like me."

Alex wasn't sure how to take that. Gypsy, despite her other faults, was attractive. She was certainly friendly.

"I pack a wallop," Gypsy said unapologetically. "It's just who I am. Most men get overwhelmed after a while."

Alex found herself wondering if she packed a wallop, too. She'd certainly put Jarett through the ringer so far in their relationship.

"Tell me about your life in the city."

"There's nothing to tell. I'm here now."

"You were in marketing."

Gypsy and Jarett had obviously had some talk while Alex had been sleeping. She shrugged her shoulders. "I was."

"So you've got a creative side."

"Somewhat."

"This is going to be a big change for you."

"It is, if I stay." She still hadn't made up her mind about that.

"You have a complicated life, my dear."

"I didn't, not until my grandmother passed away."

"So why stay here? Why not go back home now that you can sell?"

"You said it. My life is complicated. I'm not going to sit here and bare my soul to you. Suffice it to say, I have reservations about what happened to my father. I also want to know exactly how my mother died. I'm not leaving here until I get answers."

"What kind of reservations?" Gypsy asked curiously. "You said he burned up in that treehouse. We know he was at the resort to start a fire. What's there to question?"

"Would you set fire to a treehouse while you were standing inside it?"

Gypsy's lips thinned. "Well, no, I guess not. What are you saying?"

"I don't know, but something doesn't feel right."

"He didn't mention a treehouse," Gypsy reiterated. "Just the boathouse. I guess for a time, he was sleeping there. That was before he met up with your grandmother again."

That explained the old, smelly, wet clothing, the cot and the whiskey bottle.

"I'm sorry, Alex." For the first time, Gypsy actually sounded sincere. "I realize I made a bad choice when I joined forces with Butch. He described you very differently than you actually are."

"Butch didn't know me. Not ever."

"Well, I suspect that's his loss."

Alex found her heart softening. She didn't want it to. She knew Gypsy was going to be another complication in her life. That was inevitable.

"I said I'd get on the bus today and go home. I will if you want me to. Or I could stay around and give you a hand. I know you don't think I'm smart enough to be of much use to you, but—"

"I never said you weren't smart enough," Alex interrupted. She set her coffee cup aside. "I said I don't need any more distractions."

"I don't have to be a distraction. Honest, I can do lots of things. I'm good with numbers. I'm good with delegation." Gypsy went on to list her attributes.

"Why don't you want to go home?" Alex jumped to the point. She sensed Gypsy's apprehension to head back to Biloxi.

Gypsy shrugged, her shoulders rigid suddenly. "I don't have much of a home there anymore. Why do you think I hooked up with your father?"

"You have your parents."

"They're a different breed. I already told you that."

"They won't help you at all?"

"They would. But there would be strings attached. Mama is like that. Daddy is, too. I just don't want to deal with their judgment."

"Because of your failed marriage," Alex figured out.

"*Marriages*," Gypsy corrected. "They warned me not to marry the first two. When I married the last one, I didn't bother to ask their opinion. They never even got the chance to meet him. They'll judge anyway. They always do."

"They sound like delightful people," Alex said sarcastically, carrying her coffee cup to the sink.

"They're not all bad. There's love there. It's just conditional, that's all." Gypsy followed suit and washed out her own mug. "Please let me stay. I promise I won't be in the way. I will make myself useful."

Alex folded her arms over her chest and leaned back against the counter. "You realize you're a grown woman. This is a free country. I really can't stop you from staying if you want to."

Gypsy's expression turned hopeful. "You can stop me from staying with *you*. I don't currently have a job or any money coming in. What your father gave me was gone days ago."

"This isn't my house." Alex's reply was automatic.

"I know that. But you have a house of your own. Maybe I could stay there temporarily if you're not going to. I could help you go through your grandmother's things. Help you clean it up. It wouldn't be so scary then."

Alex wasn't sure she wanted anyone else going through Mimi's things. On the other hand, she wasn't sure she could handle the task by herself, either. "Let me think about it. For the time being, you can sleep at the resort. What you do during the day is up to you."

Gypsy, apparently knowing when to accept a good thing for what it was, quickly agreed.

7

Jarett took one last look around outside on the vineyard and then made the short walk to his truck. Unfortunately, before he got there, Ellery fell into step beside him. "I've been trying to find you all morning."

"I've been out here. How's Anne Marie?"

"She's doing better. Her face is still pretty messed up so she's confined to the bedroom for the time being."

"That makes things tough for Betsy at the gift shop."

Ellery sighed and shrugged. "It's getting toward the end of the busy season. September is here. We can cut hours back."

"You're going to have to hire someone else.

We need to keep the shop open, Ellery."

"I don't have time to hire someone. Besides, Anne Marie will be back at it in a week or two."

"A week or two is a long time. And you and I both know she's been dropping the ball anyway. She's always got something more important to do than run the shop."

"It's her domain," Ellery said simply.

They reached his truck and Jarett rounded on his brother. "I'm willing to keep this place going. I'm willing to keep our partnership the way it is. But I'm calling some shots now. I'm going to make a few changes. If you two can't handle that, we need to talk about dissolving things."

Ellery looked alarmed. "You don't need to go that far. I'm sure some extra help at the gift shop wouldn't upset Anne Marie too much."

"Good. I'll see about finding someone since you're so...*busy*." Jarett refrained from rolling his eyes. He knew Ellery wasn't busy at all. He'd been playing nursemaid to Anne Marie for the past few days, but that ship was slowly sailing away. Ellery only had so much patience.

Ellery frowned and Jarett knew he wasn't happy. Still, he nodded in agreement. "Whatever works. Listen, I wanted to ask you about something else."

Jarett leaned against his truck impatiently.

"No, Alex isn't selling her property to me."

"That's not what I was going to ask."

"Then what? I've got somewhere I need to be."

"Leona Grail. I heard about her bones."

Everyone had heard by now. There were no secrets in Mystery Lake. Jarett shrugged his shoulders. "Jack got confirmation."

"I just don't get it," Ellery said, perplexed. "I thought for sure they belonged to Erica Haynes."

"I think we all did, Ellery. It was a natural assumption. But Leona Grail went missing the same night."

"So what does Jack think?"

The truth was, Jarett hadn't spoken to Jack at length for days now. He'd been too busy with other things. "I don't know. Why don't you ask him yourself?"

Ellery snorted. "He'd never tell me a thing. He's not even giving Anne Marie's case much attention."

"He's got a lot going on," Jarett defended.

"My wife was attacked. I don't expect the sheriff to put her situation at the bottom of his workload."

"I really doubt that's what's happening. Jack's only one man and he's got a lot of open cases. I'm sure if you call him, he'll provide you with an update."

Ellery still seemed on edge.

"What?" Jarett asked, frowning.

"Nothing. I just don't like the way things around here are going. I don't even want Clarissa out walking around during the day anymore."

Jarett softened a little. "I don't like it, either. But hiring security was a good idea. They're on top of things. Just give Jack a chance to do his job."

Ellery nodded.

Jarett climbed into his truck and started the engine. As he drove away, he noticed his brother watching him in the rearview mirror. Ellery was getting stranger and stranger as days went by.

Blowing out a breath, he tossed the notion aside and headed for the resort.

· · ·

Alex left Gypsy at the resort that afternoon and headed into town to grab a few things. She never really had grocery shopped. She'd mostly been staying at Jarett's. She knew Gypsy didn't have a dime to her name so she figured she'd better stock the fridge at least.

Naturally, everything she did in Mystery

Lake was an adventure. She managed to come face to face with various townspeople, most of whom had a dirty look to send her way. People never changed.

Steeling herself from the scrutiny, she continued to push her cart down the cereal aisle. She really didn't know what kind of food Gypsy liked. She hadn't asked. In the end, she told herself it didn't matter. If Gypsy wanted to stare a gift horse in the mouth, she could just go home to Biloxi.

"You're still here."

She heard the male voice behind her and instantly recognized it. When she turned around, she found herself staring into Ben Haggerty's angry eyes.

The night they'd had their run-in at the diner, she'd had Jarett standing between her and Haggerty's hatred. Today, she wasn't so lucky. "Mr. Haggerty," she forced herself to say cordially.

He stared at her for a long time, his face a mask of fury. "I don't know why you don't see that the evil is here because you've brought it back with you."

Feeling tension creep into her shoulders, Alex braced herself. "I haven't brought anything back with me, Mr. Haggerty. Now if you'll excuse me." She tried to push past him.

He blocked her way entirely with his body.

"We're not going to stand for any more of this. You should know if you decide to stay, this will never be a happy place for you. Nobody is ever going to accept your presence, dead daddy or not."

"I'm sorry you feel that way," Alex managed to spit out. Again, she tried to get past him.

He used his hands this time, to stop her cart. "You may have Jarett Rhodes fooled. Hell, you may have fooled the entire Rhodes family. But I know the truth. And so does everyone else in this town. You'd best not forget that." He gave the cart a good shove and backed away.

Alex knew her hands were shaking. She did her best to stop the trembling but it was no use. The man scared her almost as much as Butch had. Taking a deep breath, she grabbed a few more items from the store, ignoring the glares of hostility she received from the people who noticed her. Then she left the market. By the time she was safely locked inside her vehicle, her nerves were completely shot. She clenched the steering wheel tightly and rested her head against it.

A thump on the window jarred her and she glanced up. CeCe was standing outside, an impatient expression on her face. She motioned for Alex to roll down the window.

Quickly getting her wits about her, Alex did.

"I called you when you were leaving the store. Didn't you hear me?" CeCe demanded, her brow furrowed in worry. "And why do you look that way? What happened?"

"No, I didn't hear you. And what way?"

"You're white as a ghost, Alex."

"I just got a little lightheaded in there, that's all." Alex expelled a breath. "What's up?"

CeCe still seemed concerned but she let the matter drop. "I'm anxious to meet your aunt, that's what. I thought maybe I could come out to the resort later on."

Alex shook her head instantly. "That's not a great idea."

"Why not?" CeCe frowned. "If you're letting her stay there, she can't be all bad."

"When I told you about that, I was hoping you'd keep it quiet."

"I didn't tell anyone, Alex. I'm just curious. She's Leona's sister." CeCe shrugged. "But I can wait if it's a big deal."

"I don't know exactly how long she'll be here. Just let me figure things out." Suddenly exhausted again, Alex avoided her friend's gaze.

"Okay, what's up?"

"Nothing's up."

"When you avoid looking me in the eye,

something's up. I saw Ben Haggerty come out of the market. Did he say something to you?"

Somehow CeCe always had a heads' up on everything. Alex shrugged her shoulders. "Nothing surprising. I really need to get going."

"He's harmless, Alex. He talks a good game but he's just an old guy with a big mouth. Don't let him bother you."

Alex saw Ben Haggerty in a whole different light but she didn't say so. "I appreciate the advice. And I'll call you later about meeting Gypsy."

"Gypsy." CeCe chuckled. "Leave it to you to have an aunt with a name like that."

Alex grinned halfway. As CeCe walked away, she exhaled in relief. Her stomach was rocking and rolling and she was having a tough time holding herself together.

Starting the car, she willed her nerves to settle down. She'd made the choice to stay here in Mystery Lake—at least for the foreseeable future. She was going to have to deal with the cons that went along with that decision.

When she got back to the resort, she saw that Jarett was there. He and Gypsy were sitting outside on the front steps, both with glasses of iced tea in their hands.

Alex stepped out of her vehicle and reached

for the groceries in the back. Jarett set his drink aside and joined her. He quickly took the bags from her and gave her a smile. That smile died gradually. Apparently he saw something in her face that he didn't like. "What's wrong?"

"Nothing's wrong. What's with people today?"

"People?"

"CeCe. I ran into her at the market." She conveniently left out the confrontation she'd had with Ben Haggerty. She knew what Jarett's temper was like and she knew he'd already had words with Haggerty once.

He relaxed a little. "You look a little peaked, that's all."

"I've had a long day." She followed him toward the house.

"I told you I'd figure out groceries for myself," Gypsy said, climbing to her feet.

"You can't buy groceries with no money," Alex pointed out.

"Well, that's the thing, honey pie. Thanks to your hunky man here, I have a job. I start tomorrow."

Alex stopped short, her eyes narrowing. "A job where?"

"I hired her to work in the gift shop," Jarett announced before Gypsy could say anything.

Surprised didn't begin to cover Alex's

reaction. *"What?"*

Jarett set the groceries on the counter. "We need help. She needs a job." He shrugged. "Seems like a no brainer to me."

Alex started to shake her head. She felt sick to her stomach again, just when she'd gotten calmed down.

"Maybe you should sit down," Jarett suggested, pulling a chair out for her.

"I don't need to sit down," she retorted, a little short of breath. "You do realize that Anne Marie runs the gift shop at the vineyard."

"I realize it, Alex. I own the place."

She continued to shake her head.

"Stop doing that," he said crossly.

"Gypsy can't work there."

"Why not?"

"Yeah," Gypsy inserted. "Why not?"

"You stay out of this. Go outside and…I don't care. Do something."

Gypsy scowled. "Don't you get me fired, honey pie. I haven't even started work yet."

"Stop calling me that!" Alex raised her voice.

"You need to calm down," Jarett said quietly. He pushed a chair under her and forced her to sit. Then he sat down next to her.

"I know you're trying to help and I love you for it. But you didn't think this through."

"I thought it through plenty," he argued. "Ellery left the hiring process in my hands. I like Gypsy. I think she's good with people. She might actually be able to unload that godawful clothing line Anne Marie shackled us with."

"When Anne Marie gets wind of this—"

"Anne Marie is out of commission for at least a couple of weeks. She's so worried about the bruises on her face that she won't come out of the house."

"Jarett—"

"Don't take this the wrong way, Alex, but you need to worry about your business. Let me worry about mine."

She closed her mouth abruptly.

"Don't get mad at me. I'm trying to help here."

"I know what you're trying to do. I just don't think you realize what's going to happen when Anne Marie finds out about this."

He shrugged nonchalantly. "She's been neglecting the gift shop for years. I've looked the other way. Not anymore. I told Ellery this morning, in no uncertain terms, things are going to change. I don't like the way things are going with the business. If he wants to remain partners..." Again, he shrugged.

She gave up, figuring he wasn't going to listen to reason.

"You really don't look good. Are you sure nothing else happened?"

"I'm fine."

"So you're not going to mention to me that Ben Haggerty accosted you at the market?"

Surprised, she met his gaze.

"CeCe called me. She was worried about you."

"She shouldn't have done that." Alex rarely got angry at CeCe but right then she was furious.

"What did he say to you?"

"Just forget about it, Jarett."

"I'll go ask him myself if you don't tell me."

His eyes told her he meant business. She tensed. "He didn't say anything that surprised me. When are you going to accept that the people in this town are never going to treat me like I belong here? This stuff with my parents— it's made everything even worse. And God only knows what Anne Marie's spreading around. Even Jack doesn't trust me."

Jarett scraped a hand over his jaw. "I don't want you going into town alone anymore. If you need something, I'll get it or we'll go together."

"So in other words, I'm a prisoner."

"*Prisoner* isn't the word I would use."

"You realize I can't live this way forever."

"I realize it. Just give it some time."

She really had no choice. "I shouldn't have sent Gypsy off outside by herself. She'll probably cause some trouble somewhere that I'll have to get her out of."

"She's fine. She met Clem and Roger earlier. They'll watch out for her."

She found it hard to believe that anyone could keep Gypsy out of trouble. "You really think her working at the gift shop is a good idea? What if she steals from you?"

"I really don't think she's a thief, despite the poor choices she made with Butch. I'm willing to give her a chance."

"You're crazy."

"But you love me." He smiled. "I heard you say it."

She had said it. In a roundabout way. "Jarett—"

"Just let me have my moment. Don't ruin it with your bullshit." He gave her a quick kiss and got to his feet. "I love you, too, by the way." He was gone before she could say a word.

8

Work on the resort was moving along nicely. Alex and Jarett took a walk around the property after dinner a couple of nights later. Just mowing the grass had made a huge difference. The campsites were all clearly visible now and the trails were easily maneuverable. Even the community firepit had been restored to its former glory.

Clem and Roger had gotten to work rebuilding the boathouse. It had framing. Another few days and it would be complete.

The only eyesore left was where the treehouse had been. The thicket of trees that had held it up were burned halfway to the trunk. The pile of rubble that lay on the ground below was the lone reminder of how Butch had died. Alex hadn't been over there. She wasn't interested in seeing what the fire had left behind.

"Your guys work fast," she remarked as they exited the trail toward the front yard.

"I told you they're good workers."

"How is Clarissa anyway?"

Jarett shrugged. "I know she was pretty upset about what happened to Anne Marie. She's been laying low. No more smoking incidents that I know about."

"It's hard being thirteen. I remember."

"I think you had a bit more to deal with than Clarissa. Granted her parents have made mistakes, but they're nothing like yours."

"I hope not." They walked up to the porch just as Jack drove up and parked his cruiser.

"Just when I thought things were starting to seem peaceful," she mumbled.

"What's he doing back?" Gypsy was there on the porch suddenly, her hands on her hips. She was glaring Jack's way.

"Did you do something that would cause the police to be on the lookout for you?" Alex asked curiously. Jarett gave her a nudge. She ignored it.

"No, I didn't. He seems hellbent on harassing me though."

Alex turned to Jack. "I've told her she can stay here at the house, just so you know."

He nodded. "I'll tell the guys." As usual, his expression turned grim.

"What?" she asked wearily.

"Is there somewhere we can talk?"

She arched a brow. "You mean alone?"

"Might be for the best. I need to discuss something with you and the fewer ears that hear, the better." He eyed Gypsy pointedly.

"Go inside," Alex told her aunt.

"But I—"

"Just go, Gypsy."

Gypsy scowled, then pivoted and went into the house.

She turned back to Jack. "What's this about?"

"I got the autopsy report back on Butch."

She braced herself. She was pretty sure what to expect. Everyone already knew how Butch had died.

"I doubt you'll be surprised to hear that the fire caused his death," Jack began. "He was burned over ninety percent of his body."

She winced. It wasn't pleasant to picture anyone dying in such a horrible way.

He folded his arms over his chest. "The other day you mentioned to me that you found it odd your father was up in the treehouse when he set it on fire."

"Don't *you* find that odd?" she asked incredulously.

"I do. I did the other day, too. I didn't have confirmation at the time, but now that I have the report from the medical examiner, I do. His death has been ruled a homicide."

She shut her eyes for a minute. She wanted to say she was shocked but she couldn't. "How do you know?" she eventually asked when she could speak again.

"The M.E. confirmed that Butch had plastic zip ties melted around his wrists. Somebody tied him up."

"And burned him alive," she finished for him.

He expelled a breath slowly. "Yes."

Her legs turned a little rubbery and she backed up so she could sit down on the porch. She struggled to mentally file this news into a compartment in her brain.

"We know the fire was started with a Firestarter stick. We found a label at the scene."

"So what's your theory?" Jarett asked, taking the words right out of Alex's mouth.

"You heard what your aunt said." Jack turned to Alex. "Butch was planning to set the boathouse on fire. I think he went over there and found your guys were there already destroying it. After that, he went searching for another target."

"The treehouse." Alex had already figured that part out.

"Yes. I think he probably ran into the wrong person. That person gained control of the situation. I can't really tell you how that happened. I don't know if Butch was already in the treehouse and someone came along and found him there, then subdued him with the zip ties, or if he was forced up there. Either theory backs up the outcome."

Alex played with the fraying hole in the knee of her jeans silently. She was at a loss again.

"This changes the scope of the investigation. I'm sure you understand that."

"It's a murder investigation now," she figured out.

"It is. I need to ask you some questions."

"What kind of questions?" Jarett asked, suddenly sounding a little less friendly.

"Routine," Jack said evenly. "I just need to know where you two were the night Butch was killed."

"You know where we were. She was at the police station. She was with you. I was down at the boathouse with Clem and Roger, helping them demo it."

"I mean after that," Jack replied carefully.

"We were here and then we went to my place. You know all this. We talked to you that morning." Jarett's voice held a note of hostility.

"I have to ask these questions, Jarett. It's my job."

"I know you don't think either one of us set Butch on fire. That's freaking ridiculous."

"Were you both together the entire night?" Jack asked, this time forcefully.

Jarett's jaw clenched. "I came back here right after the boathouse was demoed. CeCe was here, talking to Alex. We spent a very short amount of time making sure everything was locked up and then we went to my place. We were there until Ellery woke us up and told us something was on fire in the meadows."

Jack nodded, making a few notes. "I'm not accusing anyone, Jarett. I have a lot of people on my list that need to be questioned."

"Then get to it and quit harassing us."

"Jarett," Alex began, standing up.

"I don't like this at all. This mess is just getting worse and worse and you're chasing your own fucking tail." Jarett shot a disgusted look Jack's way.

"Jarett, stop." Alex set a hand on his arm and shook her head at him.

He cursed again, but he backed down.

Jack stuck his notebook back into his pocket.

Then he turned to Alex. "I should be able to release Butch's remains to you within a couple of days."

"I left all that to the mortuary." She gave him the name of the place. "Contact them and they'll take care of the rest."

He nodded. "I'll be in touch." He got into his cruiser and disappeared down the dirt road.

"I'm beginning to think you're right about him," Jarett said angrily.

"I'm beginning to think I might have been wrong. He's doing his job. He had to ask us about where we were. It's only logical that he'd come to me first." She gave him a helpless look. "Butch was my father and I hated him. He was trying to steal from me — trying to destroy my inheritance and scare me off. That's a pretty strong motive tied to me."

"You're hardly strong enough to force a man like Butch up into a treehouse and tie his hands behind his back."

"Maybe. But somebody like Mr. Shotgun would make a situation like that a whole lot easier."

He muttered an oath. "Are you trying to make yourself look guilty?"

"No. I'm telling you why I think Jack's sniffing around me. I think he's pretty sure I didn't do it but he still has to consider all the possibilities. I get that now."

"Why the sudden understanding?"

"He didn't have to give me the information about the zip ties. He could have kept that to himself—probably would have if he considered me a viable suspect."

He grumbled under his breath.

"Let it go. I think Jack and I have come to an understanding at this point. That's about all I can hope for."

9

Anne Marie stormed through the front door, fit to be tied.

She hadn't been out of the house for days. She'd been holed up in her bedroom, using every beauty regimen she could think of to improve the damage done to her face.

Finally, that morning, after being interrogated for over an hour by Jack, no less, she'd decided to check in on the gift shop. She almost wished she could turn back time and do everything she'd done that morning over again.

"Ellery!" she howled, stalking down the hallway toward the kitchen.

She found him at the table, his head in his hands. There was a tumbler of whiskey sitting nearby.

She stopped dead in her tracks. "It's not even ten AM."

He lifted his head and she figured out quickly that he wasn't on his first drink. So, they were back on that carousel.

"Before you lose your shit on me, I didn't hire her. Jarett did."

So angry she could barely see straight, she shook her head. "I don't care. I don't care who hired her. I fired her."

Ellery straightened. "You can't do that."

"Why the hell not? It's my gift shop."

"Because Jarett's going to pull out of the partnership if you do."

An ugly silence took over the room.

Anne Marie forced herself to sit down across from him. "Put your freaking drink away and talk to me."

He ignored her request. "You've been dropping the ball over there. Jarett told me that he's done messing around. We're losing money. He hired Gypsy Cowell to help out."

"She's Alexa Grail's aunt!" she yelled, loud enough that he winced.

"Yes, I met her." He took another long drink.

"How could you let this happen?"

"I didn't *let* anything happen. I've been here

at the house, breaking my neck taking care of you. Jarett mentioned hiring someone. I told him you'd be back on your feet soon but that wasn't good enough for him. He thinks you're blowing off the gift shop and we're losing money because of it. He insisted on hiring someone."

"It's not up to him to hire people to work in my shop!"

"Stop yelling!" he yelled back.

She counted to ten and forced herself to calm down. "I told her she's fired."

"I realize what you did. Jarett called me a few minutes ago and told me she's *not* fired. He's got a thing about firing the people he hires himself. Do you want to argue with him?"

"That sonofabitch!" she seethed, clenching her fists together.

"If you make trouble, he's going to end this. He's had enough."

"He's said as much before. He's all talk."

"No, he's not. I think he's dug in deeply enough with Alexa Grail that he doesn't care about this place anymore. He'll either sell his shares to someone else and we lose, or he'll expect us to buy him out, which we both know is next to impossible."

"I won't work with her."

"You don't even know her." Ellery finished

off his drink.

"I don't need to know her."

"There's nothing I can do about this, Anne Marie. Do you hear me? If you want to keep your precious vineyard, you're going to have to go along with what Jarett wants, at least for now."

"Until when?" she demanded. "How long are we going to be his hostages?"

He stared at her, bleary-eyed. "I guess until you decide you don't need this fucking vineyard to legitimize you."

She muttered a long string of curse words.

"I've heard enough. I'm going upstairs." He got up and prepared to walk away.

"I have had a very bad morning, Ellery. Don't just walk away from me and consider this subject closed."

He turned, glaring down at her. "I've had a pretty bad morning myself. The cap to it all was when Jack Frasier called me into his office and interrogated me. Would you like to know what he was asking me about?"

She bristled. So Ellery had been questioned, too. And *separately*. She cursed Jack Frasier for the second time that morning.

"Did you hear what I said?" Ellery asked, leaning over and bracing his hands against the table. "He was asking me about Butch Grail.

And do you want to know why?"

"I know why, Ellery. Just calm down."

"He was murdered. Someone burned him alive in that treehouse."

Hearing the words a second time was no easier than the first. "So?" she said nonchalantly.

Ellery straightened and snorted. "We are prime suspects, you and I."

"Everyone in this town hated Butch Grail, including his own daughter."

"That may be, but thanks to you and your vendetta against Alexa Grail, we are at the top of Jack's list."

"Me? What about you and your grudges? You don't exactly keep them to yourself."

"I don't go around town badmouthing the Grail family every five minutes. That's all *you*. Look how you're acting right now, just because my brother hired her aunt."

"I don't want to work with that woman!"

"Clearly!" He shook his head in disgust. "You're just going to have to deal with it. According to Jarett, she stays. You dropped the ball, he picked it up. You want it back, steal it from him!" He stalked out of the room, leaving her staring openmouthed behind him.

• • •

Alex was getting used to her new hours. Since work had started on the resort, she'd been getting up when Jarett did. They had a routine. He showered, then she did. They ate a light breakfast together and then both went their separate ways. They met back up at dinner and spent evenings at his house.

Gypsy had started her new job a few days earlier. Surprisingly, nothing catastrophic had happened yet. Still, Alex felt like the situation was a ticking timebomb. She knew her aunt hadn't crossed paths with Anne Marie yet. When that happened…

Driving up to the resort, Alex got out of her vehicle. She was surprised when Gypsy met her at the door, a lit cigarette in between her fingers.

"I asked you not to smoke in the house."

"It's one frigging cigarette. It's not going to hurt anything."

Annoyed, Alex glanced at her watch. "What are you doing here? Aren't you supposed to be at the vineyard?"

"Yes, I'm supposed to be at the vineyard."

Exasperated, Alex scowled. "Then what are you doing *here*?"

"I got fired."

"Fired. Already?"

"I met your friend. Anne Marie, right?"

Alex had no trouble figuring the situation out from there. "You met Anne Marie?"

"I met her husband, too. Attractive, that guy. Not as cute as his brother, but doable."

Alex shut her eyes and counted to ten. "What happened, Gypsy?"

"The husband was okay. He showed up right about when I opened the shop. He was pretty shocked to see me. I thought he was going to pass out." Gypsy took a drag off her cigarette. "He was friendly once he pulled himself together. The wife?" Gypsy shook her head, clearly disgusted. "Now that's one wound up tight broad. Rude, snotty, condescending. And she has no self-control at all. She literally started swearing at me. She fired me on the spot."

Alex easily pictured the entire scene.

"She's cold enough to freeze hot peppers on. I don't know how she managed to land herself a husband like that."

Alex heard a vehicle pull into the driveway and turned in time to see Jarett slide from the cab of his truck. He looked a little sheepish when she gave him a knowing glance.

"Shit. I was hoping I could beat you over here."

"No such luck," was all she said.

"I've already fixed things. Gypsy can head back to work."

"I don't like that woman—the hot to trot blond with the messed up face." Gypsy took a long drag. "I don't think I want to work there after all."

Alex continued to smirk at Jarett.

He ignored her. "I spoke to my brother. He had a talk with his wife. All is good."

Gypsy just arched a brow.

Alex shook her head. "I know Anne Marie very well. Nothing is all good when it's bad."

"Trust me," Jarett assured Gypsy. "I'll give you a ride back to the shop."

"What if I don't want to go?" Gypsy asked as she put out her cigarette.

"There's another dollar an hour in it for you," Jarett offered, and waited for her to reply.

"I'll get my purse." She disappeared into the house.

Jarett grinned, obviously pleased with himself.

"Why do you want her to work in the gift shop so badly?" Alex asked curiously. "It will only bring you more headaches."

He winked at her. "No, it will bring Anne Marie and Ellery more headaches. And that gives me great joy."

Alex found her lips quirking. "You're bad."

"Hey, I've done this all for the greater good. Gypsy needed a job. We need help. What's bad about that?"

Alex just rolled her eyes.

Gypsy reappeared about that time. She and Jarett headed off to the vineyard.

Alex went inside.

Today was the day. She'd been giving herself pep talks over the past month, about going through her grandmother's things. She'd finally decided it was now or never. She had boxes in her car, and she was going to show no mercy. Almost everything had to go. Only very sentimental things were staying.

Halfway through the afternoon, she was mentally and physically fatigued. Mimi had been somewhat of a packrat. In all the years Alex had lived in the house, she'd never given Mimi's room more than a mild onceover. Now that she was in the thick of things, she realized getting rid of stuff was going to be more of a challenge than she'd been expecting.

There were boxes and boxes of pictures—pictures Alex had never seen before. Some were of Mimi and her husband—Butch's father—right before and after they'd been married. Some were of a baby that Alex could only assume was Butch. There were others of Butch as he got older. His face was easily recognizable in the photographs.

The more Alex studied at the pictures, the sadder she got. It was odd that as a child Butch seemed so happy, so normal and vibrant. How had he turned into the monster he'd become?

Setting the box aside, she found another. It was filled with snapshots of Alex as a baby. There were pictures of both Leona and Butch holding her. As she perused each picture, she wished she could remember the memories. Her parents had actually appeared happy, and, shockingly, in love. Without photographic proof to spar with her own recollections she wouldn't have believed as much.

After going through one last box, she decided she needed to keep the photos, at least for the time being. Maybe someday, looking at them wouldn't feel so depressing.

Next, she went through the closet. She painstakingly packed up Mimi's favorite pink, fluffy robe. She packed up her house shoes, her blouses and pants. She boxed up the aprons Mimi had worn in the kitchen each and every time she'd prepared a meal.

The personal items were hard to part with. They were so connected to Mimi that it was as if they belonged with her wherever she was.

Alex quickly taped the box shut and marked it. Then she stood back and perused the room.

The bed was still there. She'd stripped the sheets, gotten rid of them. The mattress and box spring were old so it was probably appropriate to just take them to the local landfill.

Just as she was about to go through her grandmother's nightstand, her cell phone rang. She saw Roger's number pop up. She didn't typically get calls from Roger or Clem unless there was a problem. She accepted the call.

"Sorry to bother you, Alex, but we're down at the boathouse. We've got a couple of questions for you on how you want the shelves in here built. Do you have a minute to come down and take a look?"

"Sure, give me a few and I'll be down." She hung up and left Mimi's bedroom. Gypsy was walking in the front door just as she was preparing to go out. "You're back early. Fired again?"

Gypsy made a face. "Very funny. No. The gift shop closed early today. They're doing some kind of spraying on the vineyard. Where are you off to?"

"I'm going down to the boathouse. I need to check out some shelves. I'll be back in a little bit."

"You want me to go with you? I'm pretty handy with organization. I might have some good tips for you."

Alex didn't want any more hands in the cookie jar than there already were. She shook her head. "Thanks, but I'll be fine."

"Suit yourself." Gypsy disappeared into the kitchen.

Alex got into her car and started up the engine. She steered the vehicle toward the lakefront, where the boathouse was being reconstructed. The speed limit on the resort grounds was exclusively twenty-five miles per hour so she kept the needle there on the nose. Just as she was nearing the turn off, she hit the brake, prepared to slow down and pull into the parking area. When her foot went all the way to the floor and the car didn't slow down at all, she knew something was wrong. She pumped the brake again, her heart beginning to thud. Still, the car continued to careen toward the boat launch. The incline was just enough so that the vehicle began to pick up speed. The speedometer hit thirty, then thirty-five. She reached for the emergency brake, praying it was going to function. When she pulled it up gradually, nothing happened.

Sweat broke out on her forehead. She stared through the windshield and saw scenery starting to pass by at an alarming rate. She had no idea what to do. Another few seconds and she was going to be plummeting toward the lake.

At the last minute, she downshifted and said a prayer, turning the car away from the water and aiming for the road up ahead. If she could just stay on a steerable surface…

She felt the car slowing down but she overshot the road and rumbled into the forest. Before she could even react, the car barreled straight into a tree and everything went black.

10

Jarett stared at the clock on the wall in the emergency room. It was after six now. Alex had been back in an examining room for nearly two hours.

He was feeling frantic as hell. The minute Roger had called him and told him what had happened, he'd panicked. He'd driven like a bat out of hell to the hospital. Roger was already there. He'd ridden in the ambulance. At that time, Alex had been conscious, thank God.

"This coffee tastes like mud," Gypsy announced, offering him a cup. "But it's the best I can do. I tried to sneak into a doctor's lounge and get the good stuff but the doors are all coded."

Gypsy had shown up at the hospital pretty quickly after he had. She'd managed to wrangle herself a ride from Clem, who'd stopped by the house to let her know about the accident.

"Thanks." He took the offering but made no move to drink it.

"Nothing yet?" She sat down next to him.

"No."

"I tried to get something out of the Nazi nurse up there at the counter but she wasn't helpful. She's the one who caught me jiggling the handle on the doctor's lounge."

Jarett would have laughed if he hadn't been stressed beyond belief. Leaning over, he rested his elbows on his knees.

"She's going to be okay, honey pie. Trust me, she comes from very strong stock."

He wanted to believe that with every fiber of his being. The way Roger and Clem had both described what had happened…

It just didn't make any sense. They claimed Alex had lost control of her car and headed straight into a tree. With the low speed limit in the campground, that didn't add up. Who lost control of a car going twenty-five miles an hour?

"Anyone a relative of Alexa Grail?" a man called from nearby.

When Jarett glanced up, he saw that the man was dressed in a pair of scrubs. He was a doctor. Jarett was on his feet immediately, his cup of coffee tossed into a nearby trash can. "I'm with Alex."

"You family?"

"I'm her…" He paused. Hell, what was he? They really hadn't talked about that in detail.

"He's her husband," Gypsy announced, causing him to gape at her. "I'm her aunt."

"I'm Dr. Ketner."

"Jarett Rhodes," Jarett supplied.

"Gypsy Cowell," Gypsy threw in. "

"It's nice to meet you both. She's doing fine. We're still waiting on a couple of tests, but as far as I can tell, nothing's broken. She'll be sore tomorrow, probably more so the day after. She has a mild concussion. Barring no unforeseen issues, we should be able to discharge her in a while."

Relief washed over Jarett in waves. "Thank you for the update. Can I see her?"

"We're finishing up a blood draw. It shouldn't take long. I'll have a nurse come out and get you." The doctor headed through a pair of double doors and Jarett sat back down, his head in his hands.

"I told you she'd be fine," Gypsy said matter-of-factly.

"We're not married."

"I know how these places work. You're either a daughter, a son, an aunt, a husband, a wife—something blood or legally related. They don't give out information to just anyone."

He hadn't thought about that. "Thanks. I wasn't thinking."

"No problem, honey pie. Glad to help."

"Any word?" Clem asked, appearing out of nowhere. Roger was at his side. Both men looked worried as hell.

"She's going to be okay," Jarett informed them, feeling worlds better. "Mild concussion. A few bumps and bruises."

"Thank God," Roger said, breathing a sigh of relief. "When I saw that car barreling toward the boat ramp, I thought she was a goner."

Clem nodded in agreement. "It was pretty scary."

"I still don't understand what happened." Jarett stood up, staring from man to man. "You said you called her to come and look at shelving, right?"

"We just had a couple of questions for her," Clem agreed.

"How fast did it seem like she was going?" Jarett asked.

"I don't know. Thirty. Maybe thirty-five. It was hard to tell. I can say that I saw her face through the windshield and she looked panicked as hell." This came from Roger. "I think maybe something was wrong with the car. She didn't come to until she was in the ambulance, and by that time there were paramedics talking to her so I couldn't ask her."

"Okay, thanks. Why don't you guys go on home. We'll talk tomorrow."

Both Roger and Clem headed for the elevators.

"What could have been wrong with her car to cause a situation like that?" Gypsy asked, confused.

Jarett felt a chill suddenly. He rubbed at the sore muscles on the back of his neck as he considered her question.

"Jarett?"

Ignoring her, he reached for his phone and dialed Jack's number.

. . .

Alex stared above the gurney, her eyes glued to the tiny, brown dots that were part of the ceiling panel in her exam room.

It had been hours since she'd been brought into the ER. They'd done X-Rays, a CT scan and drawn tube after tube of blood. Now here she sat. The last time the doctor had been in—a Dr. Ketner, she remembered—he'd asked her all kinds of questions, all the while scanning the computer screen next to her bed. Then he'd left the room. He hadn't been back since.

Alex's patience was thinning more as each moment went by. Did she have some kind of terrible brain bleed or something? She had a hell of a headache, that was for sure.

She winced as she recalled the accident—the rumble as her car ran head on into a tree.

Her brakes. They hadn't been working. Her emergency brake hadn't been functional, either. She'd damn near driven herself into the lake!

Her anxiety went up another notch and she struggled to get it under control.

The door to the room opened suddenly and a nurse walked in, Dr. Ketner at her side.

The doctor was younger, probably in his early thirties. He was short and in good shape. His dark hair was shaved almost to the skin and he had a friendly smile. She'd noticed that about him earlier. He wasn't smiling at the moment.

"Ms. Grail, we've gotten the rest of your tests back. Are you aware that you're pregnant?"

The question was so shocking that she literally stopped breathing for a few seconds.

"I think we have our answer," he said over his shoulder to the nurse. "Get an ultrasound in here. Call OB."

Alex felt the room starting to spin. This was not happening. There was no way—

"I take it this is a surprise to you." It wasn't a question.

She could only swallow and nod.

"From what I can tell, it's early on, which is probably why you didn't realize it. Have you missed a period?"

Had she? She thought back, her brain so muddled she could hardly remember what month they were in anymore. September, she reminded herself. She'd been back in Mystery Lake for almost two months. Now that she was thinking about it, she realized she hadn't had a period. Not since before Mimi's funeral.

She dropped an arm over her eyes and did her best to calm her anxiety.

"Are you okay?" Dr. Ketner asked.

She lifted her arm and met his gaze. "I took a pill. That precautionary thing. It was the day after..." She shook her head. "How did this happen?"

"No birth control is one-hundred percent," he said, a sympathetic smile on his face. "If it's any consolation, your blood work's perfect. Normally we wouldn't have recommended a

CT for anyone who's pregnant but it's nothing to be concerned about. It's a very small amount of radiation and the risk is very low after a head CT."

Great, another thing for her to worry about. Had she poisoned her baby?

"Ms. Grail?" he said, reaching out and giving her arm a squeeze.

She took a deep breath and looked at him again.

"Let's just take a peek at the ultrasound before we panic. I've got OB on the way up. Can you hold tight for a few more minutes?"

She gave him a robotic nod.

"Do you want me to go get your husband? I spoke to him earlier in the waiting room. He's anxious to see you. I'm sure he'll want to be here when we take a look at the baby."

At first she was confused. She had no idea who he was talking about. Roger had ridden with her in the ambulance. "Roger's not my husband. He works for me."

"Not Roger." The doctor was thoughtful. "Jarett. I think that was what he said. I know who he is. I can just go get him if you want — "

"No!" She spoke louder than she intended. Then she swallowed again, desperately trying to rid herself of the lump in her throat. She had no idea why the doctor thought Jarett was her husband. She didn't bother correcting him. "I'd rather make sure everything's okay before I say anything to him."

Dr. Ketner gave her another nod. "Okay. That's certainly up to you. I have some rounds. OB should be here shortly." He left the room and Alex stared back up at the ceiling, a whole different set of worries on her mind now.

11

When Jarett finally saw Alex exit through the double doors in the emergency room, he sighed in relief. He jumped to his feet and closed the distance between them, pulling her immediately into his arms. "You scared the hell out of me."

She was a little stiff, and for a minute he thought maybe he was hurting her. He loosened his grip and stared down into her face. She was pale as hell. "Are you okay?"

"I'm fine. Can we just get out of here?"

"Sure.   Do you need a wheelchair or something? It's a long walk to the parking garage."

"I can go get the car," Gypsy offered,

appearing suddenly. She'd been at the coffee machine again. Apparently Alex's addiction to caffeine was hereditary.

He handed her his truck keys without much thought. She disappeared a moment later.

Turning back to Alex, he brushed some hair off her forehead so he could examine the bandage that was taped over one temple. "How bad do you feel?"

"I have the headache from hell. Other than that, I'm fine." She started walking toward the elevator.

He followed, pushing the button once they got there. "Did they give you any pain meds?"

"I'm good. I'll be fine once I get home." She pushed the button on the elevator again, as though that would speed up the slow-moving car.

He waited quietly. He had a million questions for her but he sensed now wasn't the time.

They made the trip to the front of the hospital quickly. Gypsy was there in the driver's seat. He indicated for her to hop out and ride in the back. She did so, without question.

He took them both back to his place. He'd have to give Gypsy a ride home later, once he had Alex situated.

He got her settled in his bedroom. He didn't like the pale tone to her skin, or the lethargic way she was acting. He knew enough about head injuries to know that uninterrupted sleep for long periods of time wasn't good for at least the first twenty-four hours. He told her so and she scowled at him. "I'll be lucky if I ever sleep again."

He took a seat on the side of the bed. "You want to tell me what happened?"

She snuggled under the covers, turning onto her back. "I don't know what happened. I was driving toward the boathouse and when I hit the brakes I couldn't stop."

"At all?"

"At all. My foot went straight to the floor. I tried to pull the emergency brake and that didn't work, either."

He tried to keep from reacting to the revelation.

"I finally downshifted and was able to slow the car a little bit that way. I was trying to avoid the water so I turned really quickly but I overshot the road and hit a tree." Her voice started to shake and he could tell she was getting upset. "It's totaled. My car is completely totaled."

"Don't worry about the car."

She took a couple of breaths and finally met

his gaze. "I wasn't speeding, Jarett. I wasn't doing anything dangerous. It's like something was wrong with the car."

He didn't want to scare the hell out of her but he knew he had to. "Jack has it now. He's checking it over."

"Jack?" She sniffled a little. "Why?"

There was no way to avoid telling her the truth. "Because I think someone may have cut your brake lines."

She went even whiter.

"Don't panic. The important thing is that you're okay."

"Why? Why would someone do that?" She sat up, completely alarmed. "I could have been killed!"

That realization hit him in the gut and he winced. "But you weren't. You're okay. And I'm going to make sure you stay that way. Just relax."

She leaned back onto the pillows again.

Suddenly there was a ruckus out in the hallway. Before Jarett could even react, the bedroom door burst open and CeCe stormed into the room, her face lit up with panic.

"Thank God! I was at the diner when Clem came in and told me what happened. He said you were in a car accident!" CeCe sat on the other side of the bed and reached for Alex's hand. "Are you okay? Because you don't look okay. You're white as a sheet!"

"Lower your voice," Alex said quietly.

CeCe glanced at Jarett. "*Is* she okay?"

"Mild concussion. Some bumps and bruises." He stood when he saw Jack's number popping up on the screen of his iPhone. "I'll leave you two alone to talk. Call me if you need anything." He quietly left the room. "What did you find?" he asked in greeting as he accepted Jack's call.

"Both the main brake line and then E-brake cable were cut."

"Fuck."

"Yeah. I'm on my way over there. Will she be able to talk to me?"

"She's not in great shape."

"I figured. But it's best to talk to her as quickly as possible while the accident's still fresh in her head."

"CeCe is in with her now. We're not going anywhere."

"I'll be there in ten."

. . .

When CeCe finally managed to calm down, she made herself comfortable on the bed next to Alex. "This is scary as hell, Alex. I just don't understand it."

"I don't, either," Alex agreed. Still a little in shock—for multiple reasons—she turned onto her side and looked her friend in the eye. "The last time I remember being that scared was when Erica…" Her voice trailed off.

CeCe sighed wearily. "I bet. I'm sorry all this happened. You're lucky you weren't more seriously hurt."

"I know it." Alex thought about the news she'd received at the hospital. "If I tell you something, do you promise you won't tell anyone. And I mean *anybody*."

CeCe nodded immediately.

Alex dug under the blankets and into the pocket of the sweatpants she'd put on when she'd gotten back to Jarett's house. She pulled out a strip of black and white printouts and offered them to CeCe.

CeCe's eyes grew wide when she realized what she was looking at. "No! Are you serious?" She perused the pictures closely. "For real?"

Alex nodded with a little less enthusiasm.

"Oh my—" CeCe's face broke into a huge smile. "—I can't believe it! This is so awesome, Alex!"

"Sh!" Alex hissed, glancing toward the door. Thankfully, all was quiet in the hallway. Jarett had probably gone downstairs to deal with Gypsy.

"Why do you seem so upset?" CeCe continued to study the ultrasound pictures. Suddenly she looked a little worried. "Is everything okay? I mean after the accident—"

"The baby is fine. They checked everything. I'm exactly six weeks along."

CeCe grinned again. "Does Jarett know?" Her grin dimmed a little. "It is his, isn't it?"

"Yes, CeCe, it's his."

"Well then why doesn't he know about it?"

"Because I haven't told him yet. I only found out myself a few minutes ago. I'm still trying to wrap my head around it. And I'm freaking out, if you want the truth."

CeCe handed the pictures back to Alex. "Why?"

"Why?"

"Yes, why? You're thirty-two years old. He's thirty-eight. You're adults." CeCe shrugged. "What's there to be upset about?"

"Um, maybe the fact that we just met a couple of months ago. Maybe the fact that we're not married. Maybe the fact that his family hates me. And that's just the tip of the iceberg. With everything that's going on around here right now..." Alex rubbed at her throbbing temples. "This is not a good thing."

"A baby is *always* a good thing."

Alex normally would have agreed with that statement. Right now she was too shocked, too worried and too upset to consider anything in a positive light. "I think someone may have tried to kill me today."

CeCe's eyes grew wide. "What do you mean?"

"Jack has my car right now. Jarett thinks someone may have tampered with my brakes."

"I don't believe it! Who would do a thing like that?"

"I don't know. But I can't help thinking about Anne Marie and what happened to her." Alex had been trying to talk herself out comparing the two incidents for the last few minutes but she couldn't.

"Until you know if the car was tampered with, you shouldn't stress yourself out," CeCe advised. "It's not good for you."

"Don't start treating me like a china doll. Jarett will get suspicious. So will Gypsy. I've got enough trouble with her as it is."

"I met her." CeCe chuckled. "Are you going to get mad at me if I tell you I like her?"

The truth was, Alex was starting to like Gypsy, too. There was just something about her that got under a person's skin...in a good way. "I'm still trying to get past the thing with

Butch. It's a little harder for me to appreciate her personality because of that."

"You're letting her stick around. That says a lot."

"Jarett got her a job at the vineyard." Alex managed a small smile. "In the gift shop."

CeCe outright laughed. "You're kidding me."

"Nope. She started three days ago. Anne Marie fired her this morning, the moment she realized who she was."

"She's such a—"

"Jarett pulled rank and hired her back."

"Have I told you how much I love that guy?"

Alex found her smile growing. "Yeah, he's something else."

"You need to tell him the truth. It's his kid. He has a right to know."

"I realize that. I just need to set my own head straight first."

"He's in love with you. You know that, right? And don't give me a bunch of crap about everything being complicated. All good love stories are full of complications. I'd gladly take those complications for a real love story like yours."

"What about you and Jack?" Alex realized suddenly that she hadn't been a very good friend recently. She'd been so wrapped up in her own problems that she hadn't even asked CeCe about her life.

"He's a nice guy, Alex. I like him. But he's a workaholic, plain and simple. We've spent maybe two nights together in the past two months." CeCe shrugged. "I don't want to sound needy, but I'd like a little more attention than that."

"So you broke up?" Alex realized it was nice to focus on someone else's situation for a few minutes.

"Not really. We just haven't spent any time together. He calls me. I call him. It's like we're...friends." CeCe shrugged.

Alex felt a stab of guilt. "You should probably blame me for that. Since I came back to town, I've had him running his fool head off."

"You have, haven't you?" CeCe gave her half a smile. "It's not your fault. If it's meant to be, it's meant to be. That's always been my mantra. Being in love isn't hard. Sometimes navigating its roads can be a pain, but when you know, you know."

Just then, Jarett poked his head into the room. "Jack's here. Do you feel up to talking to him?"

CeCe stood abruptly when Alex nodded. "I'll call you tomorrow. I assume you'll be on bedrest for a few days at least."

"She will," Jarett confirmed, earning himself a frown.

"I'll find you some good, juicy gossip magazines. And I'll bring you one of my world famous milkshakes and a pile of pancakes and French fries."

"Interesting combination," Alex said, shooting her a perturbed stare.

She just sent a wink in return and left.

Jack entered the room a few minutes later. He gave her a sympathetic frown. "You're really trying to take up every minute of my time, aren't you? If you weren't already with him, I'd think you were trying to get my attention." He gestured to Jarett and grinned halfway.

It was nice to see him without a scowl on his face for a change. "I don't suppose you have good news for me." She sat up in bed and propped a pillow behind her.

His grin faltered and she knew the answer before he spoke. "The brake lines were cut. Both the main and the E-brake."

She felt Jarett sit down beside her and offer her his hand. This time she didn't push it away. "I drove it this morning. It was fine on the way over from Jarett's."

"Where did you go today before you went

out to the boathouse?" Jack took out his trusty notebook.

"Nowhere. I was at the resort all day, going through Mimi's things."

"Was the vehicle parked where you could see it all afternoon?"

She thought about that. "I was in the back bedroom. Mimi's bedroom, so no, I guess not."

"Any visitors?"

"None. The only people I saw today were Clem and Roger, Jarett and Gypsy."

Silence followed her reply. Jack made a couple more notes in his book.

"What do you know about the two guys?"

"Clem and Roger?" Jarett shrugged his shoulders. "They've both been working out on the vineyard for a little over a year now. Good workers. I sent them Alex's way."

"No issues with either of them?" Jack glanced at Alex.

She shook her head. "I like them both."

He nodded. Then he was quiet again. Too quiet. She didn't like the expression on his face, either. He definitely had something swirling around in his head. "What?" she finally asked, growing agitated.

"What about your aunt?"

"What about her?"

One thick brow arched up. "She has caused

you some trouble in the past. A lot, in fact."

Alex found herself defending Gypsy right off the bat, which was a little weird. She'd been trying to get rid of the woman almost since the moment they'd met. "Why would she do a thing like cut my brake lines?"

"I don't know that she would, Alex. I'm just tossing around ideas. Somebody cut them. She's new to your situation. She's got a history of trouble making." He shrugged. "She's just an option."

"Whoever cut those brake lines had to know enough about cars to find the lines," Jarett pointed out. "Not only that, the person knew enough to cut the E-brake line, too. That's no novice to automobiles. Gypsy doesn't impress me as the mechanical type."

Jack made a few more notes. "I hear you. It was just a thought."

"Alex had a run-in with Ben Haggerty at the market yesterday."

She'd almost erased that terrible memory from her brain. When Jack looked at her, she nodded.

"What did he say to you?"

"He's had words with her before," Jarett filled in when she didn't answer quickly enough. "I stepped in and put a stop to it but he's got a problem with her being here for sure."

"I'll check into that," Jack promised. "Anyone else you can think of?"

"Every person in this town," she said sarcastically. Then she thought about Anne Marie. "Anne Marie was attacked in the vineyard the other night. That's a little coincidental. I'm not accusing anyone over there, so don't misunderstand me. I'm just saying..."

"I've already been thinking about that," Jack assured her. He shoved his notebook back into his pocket. "I don't mean to bring more bad news but your car is pretty much toast. It's evidence anyway at this point."

She'd accepted the fact that she was probably going to have to find a new car. That was the least of her problems.

"I should let you get some rest. If you think of anything else, let me know. I can see myself out," he added when Jarett started to get up. Jarett sat back down, his fingers still wrapped around hers. When they were alone, he leaned back next to her, letting her snuggle against his side.

"You should take Gypsy home," she suggested, her eyes growing heavy.

"She's fine in the guestroom for the night. I want to keep an eye on you right now."

"I'm okay. Just tired."

"You can sleep, but not for long periods of time. Don't get mad when I wake you up."

"Okay," she mumbled, already shutting her eyes. A minute later she was fast asleep.

12

CeCe stared at the television. The evening news was on. As usual, there was no feelgood story being broadcast. The station was based out of Seattle, where there was nothing but problems these days.

Flipping the channel, she scrolled until she gave up on finding anything appealing to watch. Clicking the off button, she picked up her phone. She had no missed calls, no messages from Jack. She knew he was hard at work again. The life of a cop.

She liked him a lot. She had for a long time now. She just wasn't sure she was cut out to be the significant other to a sheriff. Every day that passed, she began to doubt that more and more.

Tossing the phone down, she decided to turn in early. She had to be at the diner first thing in the morning anyway.

She took a shower and washed her hair. She stood under the water for an extra few minutes, until finally it ran cold. Then she shut off the taps and reached for her towel.

Just as she was wiping her face, a noise startled her. It sounded like…tapping.

Startled, she moved the shower curtain aside and stared out into the steamy bathroom. The door was ajar. Nothing appeared amiss.

She wrapped the towel around her and climbed from the shower.

The tapping grew louder, more precise. She realized suddenly that there was a very distinct cadence to it.

Tap, tap. Pause. *Tap, tap.* Pause. *Tap, tap, tap, tap, tap, tap.* Silence.

CeCe swallowed hard, her heart thudding forcefully inside her chest. She opened the bathroom door and peered down the hallway toward her room. She had a gun in the bedside table. Jack had taught her how to use it when they'd first started dating. If she could just get to it, she'd feel a whole lot better.

She listened for a minute, praying everything would remain quiet. When she heard nothing for a reasonable amount of time, she talked herself into believing she'd imagined the noise all together. She tiptoed down the hallway toward her bedroom, regardless. She wanted that gun.

Just as she reached the closed bedroom door, she heard the noise again.

Tap, tap. Pause. *Tap, tap.* Pause. *Tap, tap, tap, tap, tap, tap.* Silence.

Tap, tap. Pause. *Tap, tap.* Pause. *Tap, tap, tap, tap, tap, tap.* Silence.

The noise went on and on and on, until CeCe thought she might lose her mind. She whipped her bedroom door open, hurried toward the nightstand. She never made it. Something slammed against the back of her skull and she went down hard, her face smacking into the tile floor with a thud.

. . .

Alex slept off and on throughout the night. It seemed like just when she was resting comfortably, Jarett was there, telling her she had to wake up. The whole thing was very frustrating.

In the morning, she felt groggy, nauseated and irritable. She lay there for a few minutes, telling herself she wasn't going to be sick.

"Are you okay?"

She turned her head and met Jarett's gaze. He'd slept in his clothes. He was lying on top of the covers next to her, his hair mussed, his jaw littered with stubble and his expression full of worry.

She knew right at that moment that she was head over heels in love with him.

Her stomach pitched and she took off for the bathroom before either of them could say a word.

She hadn't eaten much the night before so she mostly just dry heaved. When she was done, she rested her head against the toilet and took a deep breath.

"What can I do?" he asked, stepping into the bathroom and crouching down next to her. He brushed some hair back from her face and waited patiently.

"A towel would be good."

He grabbed a towel from the counter and offered it to her.

She wiped her mouth and allowed him to help her to her feet. He didn't speak, just stepped back and let her use the sink. She rinsed out her mouth and spat, then grabbed her toothbrush from her toiletry kit and brushed furiously. She felt a little better once the awful taste was out of her mouth. When she turned around, he was leaning against the doorjamb, his arms folded over his chest. He wasn't smiling. He wasn't frowning, either. He was just watching her cautiously.

"What?" She felt a little weak so she used the counter for support.

"Is there something you want to tell me?"

She started to shake her head.

"Really. Nothing, huh?"

She narrowed her eyes.

He lifted his left hand and she saw the strip of black and white pictures he held between his fingers. "These were on the floor." He tossed them on the counter and walked away.

She stared at the space he'd vacated for a long time, completely at a loss. Letting out a curse, she followed in his footsteps and went downstairs. She ignored Gypsy and trailed him to the counter where the coffeemaker was. "We should talk."

He didn't answer her. She could tell his teeth were clenched by the tic that was popping in his jaw.

"I was going to tell you."

He rounded on her. "Before or after the kid was born?"

She flinched, caught off guard. She'd never seen his anger directed at her. Not like this. "I only found out yesterday."

"Then that's when you should have told me.

Yesterday. At the hospital. When you found out."

"I didn't get the chance."

"You had plenty of chances." He leaned against the counter, bracing his hands on the granite. He completely avoided her gaze. "Is everything okay? The accident..."

"Everything is fine. The ultrasound showed a strong heartbeat."

He was silent for a moment. Then he straightened. "That's good. I'm glad you got to hear it."

"Wait a minute," Gypsy said from across the room. "Are you pregnant?"

Alex ignored her. She kept her eyes on Jarett's. "I had no idea when I went into the ER, Jarett. I didn't even realize I'd missed a period. The time we didn't use protection, I took precautions. We've been careful every time since then. It didn't cross my mind that I could be pregnant until the doctor told me. I was in total shock."

He shrugged his shoulders stubbornly. "You had those pictures. You didn't even show them to me."

"I was going to."

"Is that why you were hiding them?"

"I wasn't hiding them. I had them in my pocket. I fell asleep last night before I had the chance to show them to you."

"Can I say something?" Gypsy asked.

"No!" Both Jarett and Alex snapped at the same time.

Gypsy grumbled under her breath but went back to drinking her coffee.

"Do you want this baby?" The way he asked the question told her he was worried about her answer. That scared her a little.

Eventually she knew she could only be honest with him. "I do."

He surprised her by relaxing.

"Do you?" she countered carefully.

"Hell yes, I do." There was no hesitation in his response.

Relieved, she calmed down significantly. "Okay. That's out of the way."

"It shouldn't be like this, Alex. This isn't the way something like this is supposed to go down. Not when we're consenting adults, in our thirties and in a committed relationship."

"Is that what we're in?" she asked. "Because we've covered some things but not that. The doctor called you my husband. I wasn't sure what to call you so I just let him think what he wanted."

"That was my fault," Gypsy intervened again. "Hospital policy. They wouldn't have given him any information without thinking he was a relative."

He scowled at her. "I can answer my own questions."

"Just trying to help," she said innocently.

"Well, don't!" Jarett and Alex both spoke at the same time again.

Gradually his lips quirked. She found hers following suit.

"See now? I've helped you get through your little spat. Kiss and make up so I can get all the details."

Alex rolled her eyes. "There are no details for you. Go find something to do so we can have a little privacy."

Unoffended, Gypsy got up from the table and walked off with another grumble.

Alex gave him her full attention again. "I'm sorry. I should have told you right away. I was pretty scared."

He leaned back against the counter. "Of what? My reaction? Because I was there when it happened, Alex. I was a willing participant."

"I know that." She shrugged and sat down in a nearby chair. "This is all happening really fast. Everything. When I came here, it was to bury Mimi—to deal with her estate. Everything has been a complete roller coaster since then. I've quit my job, moved my entire life here to a place where I never thought I'd live again. And don't even get me started on the rest of the things that have happened."

He sat down next to her, resting his head on his hand. "I realize that. But it feels right—this thing with you and me. Maybe it's the one light in the long line of darkness."

"That sounds pretty poetic."

"That's how I see it. Before you came here, I was merely existing. You've changed all that."

"I bet I have."

His lips quirked again. "There are no dull moments with you. But I don't care. I told you before, I love you. And I'll love this baby, too."

She felt emotion clog her throat and avoided his gaze.

"What?" he asked, tipping her chin so she met his gaze.

"I've never had a family. Not a real one. I mean I had Mimi, but..." She blinked as tears filled her eyes. "I'm not sure I know how to do that."

He dropped his forehead to rest against hers. "It will all fall into place. Trust me." His mouth covered hers. She leaned into him, allowing him to deepen the kiss.

The sound of his cell phone ringing interrupted them and he grimaced. "Every time, I swear."

She chuckled and backed up so he could pry

the device out of his pocket. "It's Jack." He quickly connected the call and stepped out into the foyer.

She glanced longingly at the coffeemaker. She'd read some of the information the doctor had sent home with her from the emergency room. Apparently too much caffeine during pregnancy was a no-no. The next seven-and-a-half months were going to be interesting for her.

She got up and reached for a bottle of water instead. Jarett stepped back into the room just as she was opening it. She could tell by the expression on his face that something was wrong. "What?"

"CeCe was attacked in her apartment last night. She's in the hospital."

13

It took Alex a while to talk Jarett into giving her a ride to the hospital. He tried his hardest to convince her she needed to stay home and rest. There was no way in hell she was doing that. Not when her best friend had been attacked in her own apartment.

The waiting room at the medical center was crowded. They found Jack right away. He was standing in a corner, his phone on his ear. When he saw them, he held up a finger. A second later, he disconnected his call and gave them his full attention. "You didn't need to come down here."

"Of course I did," Alex said. "CeCe is my best friend. Now tell me what happened."

"I've only gotten a little bit out of her. She wasn't completely coherent when she called me this morning." He scrubbed a hand over his jaw. "I knew something was wrong. I got to her apartment and I found the door open. She was lying in the hallway, wrapped in a bath towel."

Alex started to panic and Jack cut her off. "She's not in any imminent danger, Alex. But she is hurt." He spoke quietly and she could tell he was upset himself. "Somebody hit her in the back of the head. She's got a pretty good goose egg. They did a CT and it checked out, but they're still concerned because she's not making a whole lot of sense."

"I want to see her."

"They're not even letting me in there right now. They're drawing blood and all that crap."

"I want to see her," Alex repeated.

He and Jarett exchanged glances. Jarett shrugged his shoulders. "Might do her good to talk to someone that isn't a cop. And someone who's not her boyfriend."

Jack eventually nodded. "I'll see what I can do."

Alex waited impatiently while he went up to the desk and spoke with a nurse. He came back a moment later. "She's been asking for you. You can go in. Room 310."

Alex went down the hall in search of CeCe's room. It didn't take her long to find it. She walked inside, careful to be quiet in case CeCe was sleeping.

"Thank God! I've been asking for you for hours!" CeCe surprised her by sitting up and reaching for her.

Alex sat down on one side of the bed and squeezed CeCe's fingers. "Are you okay?"

"No, I'm not okay, Alex. She's back."

"What are you talking about?" Alex noticed right away that CeCe's fingers were cold. Ice cold. She rubbed them with her own, trying to warm them up.

"I saw her. I was lying there on the floor and I saw her."

"You're not making any sense. Calm down."

"You're not listening to me. Jack didn't, either. Nobody understands." CeCe's eyes overflowed with tears and she let go of Alex's hand and swiped at them. Then she forced Alex to look her in the eye. "I was in the shower last night. When I was getting out, I heard it."

Alex shook her head, confused. "Heard what?"

"The cadence." CeCe's eyes were wide as saucers. "I heard the cadence."

Alex stood up, taking a step back from the

bed. "What are you talking about?"

"Damn it, Alex, I heard the cadence! That freaking knock that Anne Marie made up when we were kids!" CeCe's voice had raised significantly by this point and she was trembling uncontrollably. "Don't you dare let them tell you I'm crazy! You know what I'm talking about! Tell me you believe me!"

"Okay," Alex said, taking CeCe's hands in her own. "I believe you."

CeCe, still distraught, leaned back against the pillows. "She's back, Alex. Erica. I saw her when I was lying there on the floor. I saw her and she's pissed."

Alex let go of CeCe again and backed away. Rational thought tried to convince her that what CeCe said couldn't be true. But there was another part of reality that had her thinking just maybe it was.

"Alex?" She heard CeCe calling her name. She saw her friend reaching for her. A moment later, everything around her faded away and she felt herself falling to the floor.

. . .

Jarett paced the waiting room yet again. Alex was in with another doctor this time. She hadn't been officially admitted to the hospital.

143

She was conscious, talking. She wanted to go home. After passing out on the floor of CeCe's room, she'd actually tried to walk out of the hospital without anyone checking her out.

Jarett hadn't allowed her to leave. He'd grabbed the nearest doctor, who'd convinced her to let him examine her.

"I guess I should congratulate you," Jack said, folding his arms over his chest and leaning against a wall nearby.

"Thanks," Jarett responded somberly.

"I meant that sincerely. She's got some quirks but it seems like she makes you happy."

"She's a freaking handful." Jarett raked a hand through his hair. Then he looked his friend in the eye. "But I love her."

Jack chuckled. "I guess that's the way love works."

"Did you ask CeCe what happened in there?"

"She won't talk to me. She's babbling again, not making any sense. She keeps talking about a cadence." Jack's eyes wrinkled with concern. "I'm worried they've missed something in her scans. They swear they haven't but she's got all the classic symptoms of a serious issue."

"There's nothing wrong with her."

Jarett turned in time to see Alex exit the exam room behind him. The doctor followed in her wake.

"I'm fine," she said, before Jarett could so much as ask a question.

"You're not fine. You fainted."

"I checked her out pretty thoroughly," the doctor assured him. "I think she's okay. She needs to get something to eat, maybe take it easy. She does have a concussion. Those things can be tricky sometimes."

Jarett felt immediate relief.

"We need to talk," Alex said quietly, staring from Jack to Jarett. "Here. Now."

"I'm taking you home," Jarett argued.

"I think Erica Haynes might be alive."

Jarett was stunned into silence.

Jack straightened and muttered a vile curse.

"Are you ready to listen now?" Alex turned and walked toward the cafeteria, leaving both men no choice but to follow. When they were all seated at a small table, a plate of food Alex was merely picking at in front of her, she started to talk. She looked at Jarett first. "Do you remember the night I called you? You were sleeping and I woke you up. I thought someone was outside at the resort."

He vaguely remembered the night. There had been so many interrupted nights of sleep since he'd met her, he was having a hard time deciphering them. "You're talking about the night you said someone was pounding on your door."

She nodded.

"You had a nightmare. You told me you thought it was a nightmare."

She pushed some food around on her plate, still making no move to eat it. "I was confused. I talked myself out of believing anything that happened that night was real. But now, hearing CeCe—listening to her describe what happened to her last night..." She met Jarett's gaze. "I think it was real. I told you I heard that cadence, too. And I told you I thought I saw Erica Haynes staring at me through the front window."

Jarett leaned back in his chair, at a loss.

Jack slid his cop face firmly into place. "A lot of crazy stuff has been happening since you came back to town. Traumatic stuff. Erica Haynes has been at the core of a lot of it. It wouldn't be crazy if you had experienced a very vivid nightmare."

"This was no dream, Jack. I knew it at the time. I was too scared to tell anyone because I knew I looked insane." Alex set her fork down. "The way CeCe described what happened to her—it was almost exactly the way I remember things happening to me that night."

"Nobody came into your house. Nobody

touched you," Jarett argued, silently thanking God for that fact.

"Not that night. But somebody cut the brake lines in my car yesterday."

The words hung in the air.

Jack rested an elbow on the table. "You keep mentioning this cadence. Are you talking about the secret code you had when you were kids? The one you used to get into the treehouse?"

"Where did you hear about that?" Alex asked curiously.

"I've read the Haynes file, Alex. I'd be the most worthless lawman on the planet if I hadn't after all this craziness." He was quiet for a minute. "That cadence was the reason you didn't let Erica into the treehouse, right?"

"It was the reason Anne Marie and Mercy *wouldn't* let her in," Alex corrected. "We got into a big fight about it. Mercy ended up kicking the trapdoor and the next thing we heard was Erica screaming." Alex visibly shivered. "When we looked out the window, we saw her lying on the ground below. She wasn't moving."

Jarett hadn't heard the story firsthand before. It was a very chilling tale.

"So what did you do?" Jack asked.

Alex seemed a little sheepish. "Panic. We argued some more. We were kids—stupid and immature. Anne Marie had a phone and I tried to get it from her so I could call for help." She leaned back dejectedly. "She wouldn't give it to me. I knew she had it and she wouldn't give it up."

"The famous phone," Jack said, shaking his head. "How did it end up flying out of the treehouse?"

"Anne Marie threw it." Alex avoided both their gazes. "I'm not proud of anything that happened that night. I should have helped Erica the minute she fell. I didn't. None of us did."

Both men remained silent, waiting for her to say more.

"We were all scared. It's not right, but it's the truth."

"The chances of her being alive aren't very good. You know that right?" Jack straightened. "She was a twelve-year-old child. If she did walk away that night, she would have gone home to her parents, right?"

"I don't know. We'd only just met that summer. Her parents seemed like nice people but I didn't know them well."

"Sheriff Miller has boxes of information on the case. He questioned the Haynes family multiple times. They were completely wrecked when Erica went missing. Nobody in the family drew any red flags."

"So? That doesn't mean she's not alive." Alex seemed both hopeful and terrified.

Jack, finally at a loss for words, just rubbed at his chin.

"CeCe's not crazy, Jack. Give her a chance to explain her side of this story. Trust me, it will match mine to a T."

Jack swore and hauled himself to his feet. "Okay, you win. I'll look at this from a different perspective but I can't promise you anything."

"Fair enough," was all Alex said.

Jarett stood, too. "I need to get her home. Call us when you know anything."

"Will do." Jack walked away.

Alex made no move to get up.

"Come on. It was a bad idea for me to bring you down here. You heard what the doctor said about getting rest."

"Do you believe me, Jarett?"

He jiggled his keyring in his hand. It didn't take him long to come up with an answer. "Yeah, baby. I believe you." And he realized he did.

14

When Alex got home, she found Gypsy had made her a nice breakfast of eggs, toast and some fruit. There was a glass of orange juice on the counter waiting for her, as well.

Alex wasn't all that hungry but she knew she needed to eat so she sat down and managed to get half the food down. Her stomach was a little queasy after that so she gave up and sipped her juice.

"That is one crazy story," Gypsy stated, taking a seat near Jarett at the breakfast nook. For the last twenty minutes, she'd been getting a recap on things from Alex.

"Everything that happened back then was crazy," Alex agreed, wishing like hell for a cup of coffee. She was going to have to grab some decaf. Maybe if she tricked herself into believing it was caffeinated it would do the trick.

"This girl. This Erica. Wouldn't her family know if she were alive?"

Alex had been thinking about that. She leaned back in her chair. "I know the police pondered the idea that she might have run away but I never bought into it. Erica just didn't seem like that kind of girl. We were only friends for one summer, but from what I saw, her family was loving."

"So why not look them up? Do they still live around here?"

"They were from Montana, I think. I don't remember where, exactly." Alex turned to Jarett. "Can I use your computer? Mine's over at the resort."

He sipped his coffee carefully. "Maybe you should let Jack handle this."

"I'm not doing anything dangerous. I just want to see if I can find Erica's parents."

"Alex, if that girl went home to her family, we would have heard about it. Erica Haynes is Mystery Lake's claim to fame." He set his coffee cup down.

She had to admit what he said made sense. Still... "I just want to see if I can find them. No harm, no foul."

He didn't look happy but he eventually got to his feet. She followed.

"You may be searching for a needle in a haystack. The internet will only get you so far. Do you even know what her parents did for a living? What city they lived in in Montana?"

She didn't. "Like I said, she only mentioned Montana."

Once they were in his office, he flipped open his computer and typed in a password. Then he brought up a people search. "What were their first names?"

Alex thought back. "Paul and Carolyn. They have a son named Buddy. That might not be his real name."

He started typing. She peered over his shoulder. He tried several different search engines and came up with a number of possibilities but none that could be directly linked to Erica. Paul and Carolyn were common names and so was Haynes.

He leaned back in his chair. "Jack would be able to find them faster. I can call him."

She nodded, accepting defeat. Then another thought occurred to her. "I know you won't like this idea, but I'd like to talk to Anne Marie."

He frowned. "Why?"

"I told you before, I think there could be a link between what happened to her and the brake lines being cut on my car. Now that CeCe's been attacked, too…" She let him come to his own conclusion.

He sighed wearily. "Jack told you he's considering all angles."

"He's got his hands full right now with CeCe. And anyway, I'd still like to talk to Anne Marie myself."

"She's notorious for throwing stones. So is Ellery. I doubt you'll get anywhere with either of them."

"I know how to handle Anne Marie. Just get me into that house and keep your brother out of the conversation."

Two hours later, they parked in front of Casa Bell-Rhodes. Alex hadn't been inside the main house since she was a child. Back in those days, the décor had been different and the home hadn't had an official name.

The moment she stepped into the foyer, the memories came rushing back. At one time, she and Anne Marie had been very close. They'd had many sleepovers in this house. In one instant, all that had changed.

Ellery led them into the family room. Anne Marie and Mercy were already there, seated on a plush, leather sofa. Both seemed confused and curious as Alex entered the room, Jarett on her heels.

"I heard about CeCe," Mercy said, speaking first. "Is she okay?"

"She's going to be," Alex replied. She glanced up at Jarett. "Can we have a minute?"

He arched a brow skeptically. Clearly he didn't want to leave her alone with the women.

"I'll be fine. We need to talk in private." She gestured toward Ellery.

Jarett still seemed uncomfortable but he turned to Ellery and gave his brother a gesture. "Come on."

"Why? What's the big secret?" Ellery didn't move.

"For Pete's sake, just go," Anne Marie snapped irritably.

"I just don't understand—" Ellery began.

Anne Marie cut him off. "Go, Ellery. This has nothing to do with you."

Ellery wasn't happy but he followed Jarett out of the room.

Alex waited until they were alone before she took a seat near the couch. She spoke to Anne Marie first. "How are you doing?"

"Look at my face. How do you think I'm doing?"

"It's not bad. It's healing," Alex said, for lack of anything better. The truth was, Anne Marie's face was a mess. The bruises on her cheek were a mixture of yellow and dark purple and the cut on her lip was angry and red.

"What are you doing here, Alex? I know it's not to check in on me. Ellery told me Jarett sounded upset on the phone. I assume this has something to do with CeCe." Anne Marie crossed her legs and folded her arms over her chest almost defiantly. "If you're here to accuse me of anything—"

"I think Erica Haynes may be alive."

The room grew silent.

Anne Marie's expression tightened. "That's ridiculous."

Alex had been expecting the response. She held her ground. "Awhile back, there was an incident at the resort. I heard pounding on the front door in the middle of the night."

"So?" Anne Marie prodded.

"I didn't realize at first what was happening. I'd been dreaming," Alex explained. "So I thought the whole thing was just part of a vivid nightmare."

"It probably was." Anne Marie didn't appear to be the least bit understanding.

"The pounding—it was the cadence, Anne Marie. The same cadence from when we were kids."

Mercy let out a curse.

Anne Marie's skin paled but she didn't soften her stance one bit. "You said yourself you were dreaming right before the knocking. What makes you think it wasn't part of the dream?"

"Because CeCe heard the same thing last night before she was attacked."

Mercy stood suddenly, visibly upset. Before she could speak, Anne Marie shot her a glare. "You need to sit back down. I can see you're about to panic."

"Of course I'm about to panic! You need to—"

"Sit, Mercy." Anne Marie's voice left no room for argument.

Mercy's jaw clenched. Reluctantly, she took a seat again.

Anne Marie turned back to Alex. "Just because you heard that silly cadence in your head, doesn't make it real. And it doesn't mean Erica Haynes is alive."

"I saw her in the front window. That very same night. And last night, CeCe saw her again."

This time when Mercy stood up, she didn't give Anne Marie a chance to settle her down. "I think I saw her, too. A few nights ago, hovering in the vineyard."

"Hovering in the vineyard?" Anne Marie

repeated, also getting to her feet. "What the hell are you talking about?"

Mercy, hands shaking, tried to control her anxiety. "The night you were attacked. Right after you left my bedroom, I looked out the window. She was standing near the vineyard, staring up at the house."

Anne Marie blanched. "You were upset. You probably imagined it."

"Tell her, Anne Marie." Mercy glared at her cousin.

Anne Marie remained silent.

"*Tell her*," Mercy said again, this time with more force.

The two women faced off silently. Just as Alex was about to intervene, Mercy turned and met her gaze solemnly. "She heard the cadence the night she was attacked. Someone was hammering out in the vineyard."

Alex turned to Anne Marie. "Is that true?"

Anne Marie shot a deadly stare Mercy's way. Then she glared at Alex. "I heard something. Now that I've had some time to think about things, I can't be absolutely certain it was the cadence. It was dark and I was upset."

"Last I heard, darkness doesn't affect your hearing," Mercy pointed out shakily.

"You be quiet!" Anne Marie seethed. "This wasn't your story to tell."

"It's relevant!" Mercy argued. "People are getting hurt here, Anne Marie!"

"That's got nothing to do with me!" Anne Marie shouted back.

"The hell it doesn't!"

"Okay, stop!" Alex intervened. She stood, too. "We need to calm down and talk about this rationally."

"Rationally? You're reincarnating a missing twelve-year-old. How are we supposed to be rational?" Anne Marie questioned haughtily.

"I'm not reincarnating anyone." Alex forced herself to remain calm. "I know what I saw. CeCe knows what she saw."

"And I know what I saw," Mercy added.

Anne Marie's shoulders remained tense as she sat back down. "I didn't see anyone."

"But you heard the cadence," Alex reminded her.

"Maybe," was all she would commit to.

"Somebody cut the brake lines on my car yesterday," Alex informed them both. "Right before CeCe was attacked." She looked at Anne Marie. "And right after what happened to you in the vineyard."

Anne Marie stiffened. "Your brake lines were cut?"

Alex nodded. "I managed to get the car under control enough to avoid plunging into the lake. I hit a tree instead."

As if for the first time, Anne Marie took notice of the bandage on Alex's head. She stood up again and began to pace.

"This can't be happening," Mercy choked out. "It can't."

"I've done a search, attempted to find Erica's family," Alex told them. "So far, I've come up empty. Jarett called Jack and he's going to check into that. If we can talk to them, maybe we can figure out if somehow she's alive."

"We would have heard," Anne Marie insisted. "It would have been big news around here."

Alex only shrugged. "I can't explain all this, Anne Marie. I can only tell you what the facts are."

"The facts are, I'm next!" Mercy announced hysterically. "That crazy bitch is going to come after me!"

For a change, Anne Marie didn't seem so smug. "Calm down, Mercy."

"I will not!" Mercy's breathing became labored and she got to her feet a third time.

"Sit!" Anne Marie took her cousin by the shoulders and forced her back down onto the couch. "Nobody is going to hurt you. We've got plenty of security here now. You're safe. Evie's safe."

Mercy's head continued to shake in denial.

"Stop it." Anne Marie gave her a serious stare. "We need to think straight here, not lose our heads."

Mercy turned to Alex, her green eyes full of fear.

Alex nodded. "She's right. We need to try to stay calm."

Mercy leaned over, resting her head in her hands.

Anne Marie stepped back, obviously annoyed. She turned to Alex. "If Erica is back, what's she after? Revenge?"

"That's the way it seems. Why else would all these things be happening?"

"You realize you all sound completely insane." Ellery was there suddenly, Jarett right behind him. Jarett gave Alex a helpless look.

"I told you to leave us alone," Anne Marie told her husband sharply.

"We could hear you screaming all the way in the kitchen." Ellery turned to Alex. "Whatever is going on here, I guarantee you it has nothing to do with Erica Haynes being alive, and everything to do with *your* father."

"My father is dead," Alex replied stoically, standing up. "And so is my mother, before you attempt to drag her into this mess."

Ellery's eyes narrowed. "Your aunt is still

alive. How do you know *she's* not responsible for what's been happening? And I'm still not convinced you *yourself* have nothing to do with it."

Before she could say anything, Jarett stepped in. "I warned you, Ellery. Watch yourself."

Ellery glanced at his brother with a scowl. "I can't believe you're buying into this. Erica Haynes has been gone for twenty years. Why would she come back now, after all this time, for revenge?"

Alex didn't have an answer for that.

Apparently nobody else did, either, because the room grew silent.

"I don't care what any of you do," Mercy announced, climbing to her feet. "But I'm not about to sit here defenseless with a bullseye on my forehead." She stalked toward the doorway.

"Where are you going?" Anne Marie demanded.

Mercy turned at the last minute. "I'm going to get my gun. If that bitch comes after me, she's going to get more than she bargains for."

15

The ride back to Jarett's place was silent. When he pulled into his driveway, she finally spoke.

"Anne Marie heard the cadence, too. The night she was attacked."

He didn't respond.

"Did you hear me? She heard the cadence, too. And Mercy thinks she saw Erica in the vineyard."

He met her gaze somberly. "I heard you. What do you want me to say?"

"All four of us can't be crazy, Jarett."

"I never said you're crazy." He exited the vehicle.

She followed suit before he got to the passenger side. "Ellery is wrong."

"I told you not to go over there. I warned you what was going to happen."

"Butch is dead. He's not responsible for any of this."

Jarett strode toward the front porch silently, his keys in one hand.

"Why aren't you saying anything?" She waited while he unlocked the front door.

When they were both safely inside, he finally turned to her. "I don't know what to tell you, Alex. Butch was trouble from the get-go. That makes sense to me. Erica Haynes being alive? That doesn't."

"Butch is dead!" she said again, this time a little bit hysterically. "There's no way he attacked Anne Marie on the vineyard. There's no way he cut my brake lines. And there's no way he attacked CeCe last night!"

"Calm down."

"I will not calm down!" She cursed, frustrated. "You told me you believed me."

"I do believe you. When you say you think you heard that cadence—that you think you saw Erica in the window that night—I believe *you* believe that."

She sorted the words out. "But you don't believe that's what actually happened," she figured out.

He hesitated and that was all the

confirmation she needed. She stormed toward the stairs.

"Where are you going?"

"I'm getting my bags—and Gypsy. I want you to take us back to the resort."

"Alex—"

"Don't." She sucked in some air and told herself to calm down. It didn't matter what he thought—what *anyone* thought. She knew the truth.

"Settle down. Let's try to talk about this calmly." He followed her up the stairs.

She ignored him and headed for the bedroom. Angrily, she threw her clothing back into her suitcase, along with her toiletries.

"You're being childish about this. Running away from me isn't going to change anything." He stood in the doorway, his expression full of irritation.

"I'm not running away. I'm going home. This—me staying over here—was never part of my game plan. It just happened."

He folded his arms over his chest angrily. "Game plan or not, you're pregnant with my kid. I have a say in what you're doing."

She yanked at her bag, dropping it to the floor. Then she glowered up at him. "You do not have a say in anything I do! I'm an adult woman! This is my body! Once the baby comes out, then you can have your say!" She shoved past him, ignoring the string of curses he sent her way.

She stormed down the hall toward the guestroom, expecting to find Gypsy standing there listening to their argument as though it were part of the evening news.

Instead, she found…nothing. The room was empty. "Gypsy?" she called, checking the hall bathroom. Again, the room was empty. She received no answer.

"Maybe she went back to the resort. She didn't have any clothes here. She probably wanted her stuff," he said, standing stiffly at the top of the stairs.

Continuing to glare at him, she dragged her bag down the hallway. When she reached the stairs, he easily maneuvered it from her hands and gestured for her to go ahead of him.

Scowling, she did. When she reached the first floor, she took a good look around, making sure Gypsy wasn't in the house somewhere. Then she glanced outside. Still, there was no sign of anyone.

Her chest tightened a little as that all familiar feeling of dread settled over her. "Something's wrong."

"Nothing's wrong. She went back for her clothes. She mentioned earlier that she needed them." He set her suitcase down, still frowning at her. "If you want to calm down, we'll drive over there and make sure."

"Bring the bag," she told him, moving toward the front door.

He cursed and followed her.

The ride to the resort was brisk. When they reached the front yard, she hopped from the truck and used her key to enter the house. She stopped dead in her tracks once her feet hit the hardwood just inside the front door.

There were papers strewn from one end of the dining room table to the other. Mimi's financial papers. There were bank statements, bills and finally, a copy of the will that Spenser Malin had given Alex the day she'd agreed to take control of the resort.

Stunned, she stared at the mess.

"Did you leave the place this way?" Jarett asked, gently moving her aside and stepping into the house.

"No," she said quietly.

He went through the house, room by room. With every moment that passed, she began to feel more and more anxiety.

When he returned to the living room, his expression was grim. "She's not here. Her clothes are gone, too."

She turned back to the table, shaking her

head.

Jarett was already on the phone to Jack.

By the time he arrived on the scene, Alex had wrapped her head around the reality that her aunt, like every other member of her family besides Mimi, had likely betrayed her—for the second time, no less.

"Have you tried calling her?" Jack asked curiously.

"She doesn't have a cell phone."   Alex sat down on the couch, ignoring the pounding that once again, had begun to commence behind her temples.

"When was the last time you talked to her?"

"Late this morning. She was here when we got back from the hospital," Jarett replied. "We left to go to the main house for a bit. When we came back, she was gone."

"Has anyone else seen her today?"

"I called the gift shop. She was supposed to work at one. She never showed."   Jarett jammed a hand through his hair.   "This is all my fault. I talked Alex into letting her stay. I thought she was legit."

Jack remained somber. He glanced at Alex. "You're awfully quiet. What are you thinking here?"

"She's a fraud," she admitted. "That's the only explanation."

Jack let out a sigh. "Okay. She didn't break any laws here. You allowed her to stay in the house. The fact that she went through your private papers isn't really any reason for me to go after her. Not only that, it's really not that alarming. It's just financial information, right? She didn't steal any money or take anything valuable."

"No." Alex thought about Ellery—about the accusations he'd tossed at her earlier. "What about the car? The brakes? And what about Anne Marie and CeCe?" She started to get a very bad feeling and tried to keep it from swallowing her whole.

Jack sighed. "I've got no real proof. And I'm struggling for a motive here. She doesn't stand to gain anything from your death. She really has no reason to attack Anne Marie or CeCe, either. Besides, she was in jail when Anne Marie was attacked."

"That's right." Still confused, Alex tried to sort through the facts.

"Did she say anything odd to you before you left for the boathouse yesterday?" Jack asked.

Alex considered that. "She offered to go with me." She met his gaze. "She gave me some story about how good at organization she is. I was supposed to be looking at shelving."

"Why would she do that if she knew the

brake lines were cut?" Jarett pointed out.

"Exactly," Jack agreed.

Alex wasn't sure what to think. Her head was spinning in a million different directions. She didn't want to believe Gypsy was up to something—that she was responsible for what had happened the day before with the car. But nothing made any sense. Why had she just taken off?

"I'll have my guys out searching for her. She can't have gotten far without a vehicle." Jack lifted his phone as he strode toward the front door. "By the way, I had one of my deputies do some checking. Erica Haynes is still listed as a missing person. She never made it back to her family."

Alex accepted the news with as much dignity as she could manage. "Did anyone actually talk to her parents?"

Jack seemed conflicted. "This is a very touchy subject, Alex. These people lost their daughter twenty years ago. I want to be careful about opening up old wounds for them without concrete proof that it's necessary."

She couldn't really fault him for that.

Once he was gone, Jarett joined her on the couch, his elbows propped on his knees. "I'm sorry."

"Don't apologize. It won't help anything.

I'm the one who let Gypsy out of jail. I didn't have to."

"Not for that. I'm sorry for all the things I said earlier — about you — about the baby."

She met his gaze. He appeared genuinely sincere. "You didn't say anything that bad."

"I'm not trying to call you crazy. This whole thing is just so out of control."

"You're telling me. Do you think Gypsy's up to something?"

"Do you?"

"I don't know. I can't figure out why she'd be going through my papers — through Mimi's papers. She stands to gain nothing."

He contemplated that. "She didn't steal anything. Not from here, not from my place. Not from the gift shop."

Alex wasn't sure what to make of that fact, either.

Jarett just sighed wearily. "She seemed happy this morning, Alex. About the baby. About everything."

Alex had noticed that, too. Still… "We don't know her. I tried to point that out to you when she first turned up. She's a stranger to me. I should have been more careful."

"*I* should have been more careful," he corrected. "I really thought I saw something good in her. So much for my psyche degree."

Wearily, she got to her feet. "She took her key. The one I gave her. She may try to come back."

He peered at the mess on the table. "She's already seen the papers. Is there anything else you're particularly worried about?"

She realized there really wasn't. Everything Mimi had was more sentimental than valuable. They cleaned up the mess and he carried the banker box full of papers to his truck. By the time they got back to his place, Alex was exhausted. The minute her head hit the pillows, she drifted off to sleep.

16

Jarett waited until Alex was asleep. Then he went down to his office and took a seat behind his desk. The first call he made was to security. He made sure they were aware of the fact that Gypsy was AWOL. He made a quick security code change for the system at the gift shop. Then, he had no choice but to call his brother. Naturally, Ellery was ecstatic to be right for a change.

"You never should have hired that lunatic."

"I don't need to hear you say I told you so. For all I know, Gypsy could be halfway back to Biloxi right now simply because she missed her family."

Ellery snorted. "Keep telling yourself that."

The call ended promptly at that point with Jarett cursing under his breath. He lifted the screen and waited for his laptop to boot up. When it finally did, he typed in the name Erica Haynes and watched as the small circle in the corner rotated quickly.

A minute later, he found himself staring at a tiny, blond girl with curly hair and big, brown eyes.

Erica had been twelve years old at the time of her disappearance. While the tragedy had occurred over twenty years before, there were plenty of articles on the incident. Jarett went to work scrolling through them. One after the other, he read, filing away fact after fact.

The entire story Alex had already relayed to him was there in black and white. It all checked out. Erica had climbed up to the treehouse to meet the girls. Eventually she'd fallen. Then she'd seemingly vanished into thin air.

Leaning back in his chair, Jarett thought about that. If the kid had fallen—was seriously injured—she wouldn't have been able to get up. Alex had admitted the girls had argued—hadn't gotten Erica help promptly. He estimated that left a good five-minute window for her to have regained consciousness and left the scene.

Or for someone else to have found her and taken her. But who? And why?

There were a lot of unanswered questions hanging in the air.

He glanced at a picture of Paul and Carolyn Haynes, taken just after their daughter had disappeared. As he perused the photo, read the caption underneath, he discovered there was some background information listed. Paul Haynes had been an attorney. His wife had worked as a law clerk. They were based out of Helena, Montana.

His curiosity piqued further and he tapped on the keyboard. A moment later he was staring at the website for Hamner, Haynes and Lormer, Attorneys at Law.

The law firm specialized in criminal law. The partners were listed. Paul Haynes was one of them. Jarett clicked on his name and read the brief biography that popped up.

Paul Haynes had been practicing law since 1991. He and his wife Carolyn had been married for thirty-six years and shared three children. They were active in community affairs — including multiple missing and exploited children charities — and loved to travel.

That was it. There was a family picture next to the biography that Jarett only glanced casually at before scrolling back.

He spent another few minutes searching and

managed to locate an obituary. It was for Carolyn. She'd died in 2019.

Sighing, he leaned back again. The picture in the obituary was a nice one. Carolyn Haynes had been attractive—far too young to be gone at fifty-three.

He could only guess what her cause of death had been because there wasn't one listed. At the bottom of the page the family asked for donations to a cancer organization in lieu of flowers. That said a lot right there.

He scrubbed his hands over his face and stared up at the ceiling for a long time.

He really didn't know what to think of things. The story Alex was sticking to—her theory about Erica Haynes—it was impossible…wasn't it?

He reminded himself that both CeCe and Anne Marie had heard the same cadence just before they'd been attacked. And then there was Mercy and her claim that she'd seen Erica in the vineyard. Something was definitely off here. He just couldn't figure out what.

. . .

When Alex opened her eyes, it was morning. Surprisingly, she'd slept soundly through the night.

Turning over, she realized right away that Jarett wasn't there. When she checked the clock, she saw that it was after nine. She'd slept for nearly twelve hours.

Stretching, she slid out of bed. She was glad to note that her headache was gone finally. She felt a little nauseated but she figured that was probably due to the pregnancy, rather than the concussion.

She took a shower and dressed, then went downstairs where she found Jarett sitting in front of his laptop at the kitchen counter. He smiled when he saw her. "Good morning."

"Good morning. You must have gotten up early."

"I did my morning walk around six. I like to start my day that way." He gestured to the counter. "I grabbed some decaf from the gift shop. I noticed you haven't been drinking your coffee so I googled it. I know decaf isn't the same but..."

She closed the distance between them and gave him a firm kiss on the mouth. "Thank you."

"You're welcome," he said, chuckling. "I had a feeling you were going to be pretty bummed about the coffee thing."

"Seven months and counting," was all she said, taking a seat at the nook and resting her elbows on the granite.

"Do you want me to make some?"

"Hold off for a bit. My stomach's a little iffy."

He gave her a sympathetic look. "I'm sorry. You want me to make you some breakfast?"

"Maybe in a while. Have you heard anything from Jack?"

"He called earlier. CeCe is at his place. He doesn't want her going home for the time being."

"Is she doing any better?"

"She's still upset. She's sticking to her story."

Alex wasn't surprised. She was sticking to her story, too.

"Listen, I stayed up last night after you went to bed and did a little sleuthing. I didn't find out anything monumental, before you get too excited. But I did find out that Erica's mother died in 2019. Her father is still alive. He lives in Helena. He practices criminal law there."

She perked up instantly. "Is there a phone number for him?"

"There is. But I think you should settle down before you even think about using it."

"I am settled down."

"Jack's right, Alex. Erica's still listed as a missing child. All the articles I've come across talk about her disappearance and what the family has gone through over the years. They've been active with several missing and exploited children charities."

Alex had to admit that didn't sound hopeful. "I still want to talk to him."

"I figured you would. But I think you should be very careful what you say. The guy's been through enough. And now that his wife is gone, too…" He shrugged his shoulders. "You get my drift."

"I do."

He slid a piece of paper across the counter toward her. "His office number is the only one I could find."

She took it gratefully. "Thank you."

"You're welcome. Now about Gypsy…"

"What about her?"

"I've been thinking. Something's smelling pretty fishy here."

"You mean her taking off out of nowhere."

He nodded. "I don't get any of this. I'd really like to know if she went home."

She thought that over. "There's no way for me to find that out. I don't know exactly where her home is."

"Biloxi."

She frowned. "Yes, Biloxi. At least that's where she's from. That doesn't mean that's actually her home."

"It's a starting point. Didn't you say your grandfather is a banker?"

"He *was* a banker. He's got to be in his seventies now at least. He's probably retired."

He slid another number her way. She started to shake her head.

"If she's there, we know she's home. If she's not…"

"It's barely been twenty-four hours. She could be anywhere."

"Maybe she's contacted her parents. With no money and no car, she'd have to have some help getting back to Mississippi."

"I'm not calling them, Jarett." She stood defiantly.

"Okay. It was just an idea."

"I really think she just split anyway. She's a flake. You saw that. I tried to warn you about her."

"I know you did." He shut his laptop.

"But you still think there's more here than we're seeing clearly."

He shrugged and nodded. "The fact that she didn't even wait around for her paycheck is interesting to me. She had no money, yet she didn't steal from any of us. She was happy as hell here, yet she vanished into thin air."

"So why was she going through my stuff—

digging through Mimi's paperwork?"

"I can't explain that. Not yet."

She didn't want to deal with the doubt that sprang instantly into her head.

"I'll leave you alone to make your call. I have some stuff to deal with in the office." He dropped a kiss on her forehead and left the room.

Alex stared down at both the phone numbers she held in her hands. Eventually, she set the one for Gypsy's parents aside. She lifted her phone and dialed Paul Haynes' office.

"Hamner, Haynes and Lormer," the receptionist said perkily in Alex's ear a moment later.

"Hi, I'm trying to locate Paul Haynes."

"May I ask who's calling please?"

She hesitated. She wasn't sure if Mr. Haynes would remember her or not.

"Hello?" the woman asked.

"Alexa Grail," she eventually admitted.

"Is this regarding a legal matter?"

"No, not exactly. This is personal."

"Oh, I see. Well, Paul isn't working today. He's in on Wednesdays and Thursdays. I can leave a message. Is there a number where he can reach you?"

Alex rattled off her cell phone number and hung up, disappointed. It was only Monday.

She was going to have to wait a couple of days at least before Paul Haynes would get her message.

She skimmed the other number Jarett had written down, her stomach clenching.

She had to admit, she had reservations about Gypsy's sudden departure, as well. But did she really want to open up this can of worms?

She went back and forth for a while. Every time she had herself convinced Gypsy had hit the road on purpose, with something awry on her mind, a niggling of doubt came creeping back up and she started the process of thinking about the situation over again.

Finally, she bit the bullet and entered the number into her phone.

"George Cowell," a male voice answered a few seconds later.

Alex froze. She wasn't sure why but she hadn't expected anyone to pick up her call right away. And she certainly hadn't expected her grandfather to answer himself. Wasn't this an office number?

"Hello?" Cowell repeated impatiently. "Who's there? Gypsy? Is that you?"

Caught off guard, Alex inhaled and held the breath.

"Damn it, girl, you can at least speak if you're going to call. What the hell is wrong with you?"

Alex cleared her throat, then forced herself to say something. "It's not Gypsy. My name is Alexa. Alexa Grail."

Dead silence followed her announcement.

"I think I'm your granddaughter," she added, when he didn't say anything.

"I know who you are."

Alex was caught off guard again. "Okay," she eventually said.

"How can I help you?" he asked, as though she were calling with a random business question.

Getting her bearings back, she kept her voice neutral. "I'm not sure that you can. I'm trying to find Gypsy."

He didn't answer right away. When he finally did, he sounded perplexed. "Why would you be looking for her?"

"Because she was here, staying with me. Now she's disappeared and I'm concerned." There, that sounded good. And it was mostly true.

"Where is *here*?" he asked.

"In Mystery Lake, Washington."

She heard him grumble an oath. "What in the hell is she doing there?"

That was a story she really didn't want to get into. "I take it you haven't seen her?"

"No, I have not. Not for months now. We haven't gotten so much as a telephone call from her. I'm not sure what your game is but I should let you know, we're not wealthy. If that's what you're after —"

"You think I'm calling you for money?" Alex tried to keep the emotion out of her voice.

"I can't think of another reason you'd be calling out of the blue like this. Unless…" He paused again. "Has your mother put you up to this?"

Alex didn't like the accusatory tone to his voice. She cleared her throat. "No, sir, my mother hasn't put me up to this. She's been dead for twenty years. I'm sorry. I shouldn't have bothered you." She disconnected the call, a cold feeling in her heart.

When the phone began to ring a minute later, she saw that George Cowell was calling back. She hit the silence button and sent the call straight to voicemail. She'd gotten all the information she needed from him.

17

Alex had been quiet for most of the day. Jarett had worked from home, in his office. He'd come out and made them both lunch, which she'd eaten. But he could tell something was bothering her.

By dinnertime, when she was still eerily silent, he gave up on respecting her space. "What happened?"

In the middle of chewing on a piece of lettuce, she gave him a quizzical stare.

"You haven't said two words to me all day."

"I'm sorry. I've had a lot on my mind."

"How about sharing whatever that is with me." He waited patiently.

"It's nothing about Erica. I called her father's

office. He's out until Wednesday."

"Okay." He waited for her to say more.

"You're going to force this issue, aren't you?"

"No, I won't force it. But I am still concerned about Gypsy. Jack hasn't found her. Things aren't adding up here."

"She's not in Biloxi."

"How do you know?"

"Because I called her father." She set her fork down.

He realized right away that whatever conversation she'd had with George Cowell hadn't gone well. "What did he say?"

She shrugged. "The conversation lasted all of five minutes. Not much."

"Not much?"

She looked him in the eye. "He asked if I was after his money. Then he asked me if my mother put me up to the call. He didn't know about her death. He does now."

Jarett winced. He immediately felt the urge knock the crap out of George Cowell, old man or not.

"It's not a big deal, Jarett. I didn't anticipate the conversation going very well. I did learn that he hasn't seen Gypsy in months. He had no idea where she was, or who she was with."

"Shit."

She remained silent.

He bit back another apology. He'd been doing that with her far too much lately and he knew she had to be getting tired of it. "He doesn't know you, Alex. He's probably just a bitter, old bastard."

"Maybe. He knew who I was. When I said my name, he knew."

He let out a sigh. He'd really done it this time. "Do you want to hear me apologize again? Because I am sorry. I had higher hopes for him."

"No, no more apologies." She lifted her head. "But I want you to remember something. You and I had very different childhoods. My family—they aren't like yours. Mimi was the only good I've ever known."

He had to admit it was starting to seem that way. "Okay. I'll keep that in mind."

They finished eating in silence. Then they drove over to the resort to check on things. Clem and Roger had resumed their work. The boathouse was nearly finished. The campsites were improving every day. The sprinkler systems were back up and running so everything was turning green again.

"It's coming along," Jarett remarked, pulling up in front of the house.

"It is."

They checked around inside to be sure everything was as she'd left it. Once they deemed that it was, they drove back to his place. Alex was surprised when they found Mercy on Jarett's front porch, alone. She stood when they approached. Alex could see the apprehension in her eyes—the fear. She was obviously on edge, not that Alex could blame her.

"Can we talk?" she asked, turning to Alex pointedly. "Alone?"

"Sure," Alex said unsurely.

"I'll be inside if you need me." Jarett disappeared into the house.

Alex took a chair near Mercy's. "What's up?"

"I'm scared to death, that's what's up." Mercy bent over and rubbed her hands over her face wearily. "I don't eat, I don't sleep. I can't let Evie out of my sight for even a minute, so I haven't been to work in two days. I'm probably going to lose my job." Mercy shook her head. "I don't know what to do anymore."

Alex felt sympathy for her old friend, even though they really weren't friends anymore. "I'm sorry, Mercy."

"How is CeCe?"

Alex had spoken to CeCe earlier that afternoon. "She's doing okay. She's with Jack."

"I figured." Mercy stared out at the rolling hills that backed up the Bell-Rhodes estate. "I'm thinking about packing up — getting out of here. Evie and I have ties in Portland and Seattle. We may head one way or the other. I don't know yet. I just know I can't stay here."

"Jack's going to get to the bottom of this. It's a matter of time."

"I've never gotten over it, Alex. The whole Erica thing. The truth is, I want nothing more than for her to be alive. Then maybe this guilt I've had for so many years will go away. It eats at me daily like a cancer. That's half the reason I thought I imagined her in the vineyard the other night." She met Alex's gaze. "I've been seeing her face everywhere since that freaking night when she fell from the treehouse. I know it was my fault." She let out a curse and leaned over, staring at the ground. "I was awful back then. Just horrible. If Evie ever behaved that way..."

Alex was surprised to hear the confession. As long as she'd known Mercy, there'd never been any indication that she had a conscience. Even back when Erica had first disappeared, everything had always revolved around Mercy and Anne Marie and what was best for them.

"I know what you're thinking. And I don't blame you. I have no real excuses. The kid thing will only take me so far. To this day, Anne Marie hasn't changed one bit. And I still play her game. When she was cheating, I covered for her. When she tells me to keep a secret, no matter how big that secret is, or who it affects, I still keep it." She shook her head. "I guess it's because she's been the only constant in my life since I lost my parents. Without her…"

"You don't have to explain anything to me."

"I don't trust her."

Alex narrowed her eyes. "Anne Marie?"

Mercy nodded. "I've had doubts about her for a while now. Ellery, too. There's something off there."

"What do you mean?"

"I mean, she came to me the other night and told me about hearing the cadence just before she was attacked. She made it this big secret that I couldn't even tell Ellery—or Jack. Then when you approached her…well, you saw how she reacted."

Alex wasn't sure what to say.

"It's not just that, either. This whole battle she's got going with Ellery has gotten completely out of control. He cheated, she cheated. They both walk on each other constantly, treating each other like crap. I watch them and it makes me sick to my stomach. Yet they continue to stay together, for monetary reasons. They don't want Jarett to gain majority control in the vineyard."

Alex knew all about that.

"I just have a bad feeling, Alex. About everything."

Alex had a bad feeling, too. "Have you told Anne Marie you're going to leave?"

Mercy shook her head. "I haven't completely decided yet. My ex-husband—he's been calling me recently about recharging his relationship with Evie. I'm considering his request. I need to figure that out before I decide anything else."

"I don't know that this will make you feel any better but I've located Erica Haynes' father. He lives in Helena. He's an attorney."

"Just her father?"

"Her mother passed away two years ago."

"Have you spoken with her dad?"

"Not yet. I left a message. He only comes into the office on certain days of the week."

Mercy bit her bottom lip. "I searched online. I couldn't find any indication that Erica found her way back home. All the sites imply that she's still a missing person."

"That's what I found, too. Jarett's the one who located her father."

"I wonder if he'll remember you. Erica's

dad, I mean."

"I have a feeling he might, not that that's a good thing."

"Yeah," Mercy agreed, sighing. "I should go. I just felt like I should warn you about Anne Marie. I'm not sure what she's up to at this point but she's been acting weird as hell. So has Ellery. There's trouble brewing there. You know they both want your land."

"I know it. Neither of them will be getting it."

"So you really are going to stick around?"

Things had definitely changed in her world. With the baby on the way, Alex knew her relationship with Jarett was going to be front and center for her. She didn't go into detail with Mercy. "That's my plan," was all she said.

"I heard about the baby. I guess congratulations are in order."

Alex was surprised. The only person she'd told about her pregnancy was CeCe. She figured CeCe had been pretty tied up since she'd found out. So who had told Mercy? And how had that person heard the news?

"Jarett told Ellery," Mercy said in explanation, getting to her feet. "I'm not trying to rat him out if you weren't ready for the news to get around. I, for one, think it's a great thing. Jarett's a good guy. If he had ever given me a second glance..." She shrugged sheepishly. "Well, let's just say my life would probably be a lot different right now."

Alex didn't take offense to the words. She stood. "Do you want Jarett to walk you back to the house?"

"I'm in the guesthouse. I couldn't take any more of Anne Marie and Ellery at close range." A smile threatened and she lifted her hand in a small wave. "It's plenty light out. I'll be fine."

Alex watched her walk across the grass. She waited until Mercy disappeared around the corner of the guesthouse before she went inside. She found Jarett in his office, sitting in front of his computer.

"Dare I ask what that was all about?" He arched one dark brow.

"As you can imagine, she's upset. Scared. She's worried about her daughter." She leaned against the desk. "She's not who she used to be. Her relationship with Anne Marie will most likely always conceal that fact."

"Most likely," he agreed.

"She doesn't trust Anne Marie and Ellery."

"Who does?" he asked, scribbling his signature on a piece of paper. "Your cell phone has been ringing non-stop for the past half-an-hour." He gestured to a corner of his desk where her phone was lying. "You must have left it in here earlier."

She glanced at the screen. She saw four missed calls, all from George Cowell. He'd left no voicemails, she discovered.

Jarett tossed his pen down and leaned back in his swivel chair. "You planning to talk to him?"

"I thought we agreed you were going to respect my feelings about my family and stay out of things."

"We did. But he's being pretty persistent. Maybe you should hear him out."

"Why? So he can accuse me of trying to extort money from him again?" She pocketed her phone.

"Okay, your decision," he said, backing off.

"Did you tell Ellery about the baby?"

"Yes."

"Why?" She couldn't hide her annoyance. She'd planned to keep things quiet deliberately. It was still early on and she was just getting used to the idea of being pregnant herself.

"Because, Alex, I wanted to make sure he knows to keep his distance. I'm not about to deal with any of his bullshit. Not when it comes to you."

"You should have warned me. Mercy knows now. Anne Marie knows."

"Is it some kind of secret?" He frowned.

"We've come to an understanding, you and me. Everybody will find out sooner or later."

"The people in this town don't like me. You're opening up quite the can of worms."

Anger flashed in his eyes. "Is that what you're worried about—what the people in this town are going to think?"

"I haven't left the resort except to go to the hospital or come here to the vineyard in days. There's a reason for that. You keep saying I'm not a prisoner but that's how I feel."

"It's temporary. People will get used to you."

"Really?"

"They'd better," was all he said.

"You can't protect me around the clock."

"Watch me."

He was stubborn as a mule when he wanted to be. Giving up on arguing with him, she left the room and got her own laptop from the bag of stuff she'd brought over from the resort earlier. Carrying it into the kitchen, she sat down at the counter. Before she had time to boot the machine up, her phone rang again. This time it was Jack calling. She answered immediately.

"I thought you'd want to know," Jack said once they'd greeted each other. "I've got confirmation about your mother—about when she died."

She braced herself. "Go ahead."

"Estimated time of death was twenty years ago, just like our M.E. thought. Cause of death stands."

"So no surprises," she figured out.

"Not at this point."

"I appreciate you letting me know."

"No problem."

"How's CeCe doing?"

"She's good. Pain in the ass. She doesn't want to rest. I'm about to hogtie her."

She chuckled at that. "Good luck."

"Yeah, thanks." He hung up.

She set her phone down. Now that she knew for sure her mother had been murdered twenty years earlier, she still didn't feel any relief. There were always going to be doubts in her head about her mother's intentions. Had Leona been running away? Had she deliberately left Alex behind?—with an abusive father, no less. Had she loved her daughter at all?

These were questions Alex longed to have answers for and she feared deep down that she was never going to get them.

18

Anne Marie finished clearing the dinner dishes. She and Clarissa had eaten alone. Ellery hadn't been home all day. She had no idea where he'd gone off to. She'd called his cell phone and it had sent her straight to voicemail.

She was getting tired of his antics. They'd made a pact to work things out and he wasn't making much of an effort at all. He'd already missed one of their family counseling appointments. He was distant and uninterested when he was around, unless he was in the mood for sex. It was like he'd just flipped a switch again and didn't give a damn. The only good thing about him was that she hadn't noticed him drinking much. She had to thank

God for that favor.

Hearing the back door open, she lifted her head in time to see him walk in. He was dressed casually, in dirty, old blue jeans and a sweatshirt.

"Where the hell have you been?"

He glanced at her as he washed his hands. "Out."

"I realize that." She slammed a stack of plates down on the counter. "Out where?"

"Just out, Anne Marie. Working."

"I asked around. You weren't on the vineyard today."

"I was down in the cellar, if you must know. I was doing some inventory."

"I checked the cellar, Ellery." She glared at him. A very strange feeling began to creep up on her.

"There's no way you searched the entire cellar. That would take you all day." He dried his hands. "Just don't worry about what I was doing."

"I am worried." She put her hands on her hips. "What's going on with you? I thought we had an agreement."

He tossed the towel down and met her gaze. "You mean the agreement where we band together to keep my brother from screwing us both? Yes, we do. What does that have to do with where I've been today?"

Her scowl grew deeper. "Are you still upset about the other day—about Jarett's little announcement?"

Ellery hadn't been happy at all when he'd learned of Alex's pregnancy. He'd ranted and raved for hours. Hell, Anne Marie had done the same thing. This baby was hardly good news for them. It only strengthened the possibility that Alex was here to stay—that she and Jarett were going to be joining forces permanently.

"Little announcement?" Ellery snorted. "They're as good as married, Anne Marie. Any chance we had of getting our hands on that property died and went to hell."

"We've still got this place."

"*Half* of this place," he corrected. "Are there leftovers?"

"In the fridge," she snapped, frustrated.

Ellery dug out the pork chops she'd made for dinner and dished himself up a plate. He added some mashed potatoes and a pile of carrots to the mix. He had one hell of a healthy appetite for someone she feared was about to self-destruct.

"I'm worried about you," she finally admitted.

"I've stopped drinking. I'm here. What's there to worry about?" He shoveled in a large bite of food, avoiding her gaze.

"You missed our appointment yesterday. With the counselor."

"Sorry. It slipped my mind. I've been thinking and I'm not sure the counseling thing is necessary anyway. What's the point?"

"The *point* is that we need to straighten things out for Clarissa's sake."

Ellery stopped eating and set his fork down. "This is never going to be the perfect family. You realize that, don't you?"

"*Perfect* is a far cry from what I'm going for. I just want *tolerable*."

He thought about that. "I'm here. You're here. We still have our business. Clarissa's not smoking or burning anything down. My brother isn't kicking my ass. I think that's probably as tolerable as it's going to get around here." He turned around and walked away, carrying his dinner with him.

So angry she wanted to punch something, Anne Marie shoved the dirty dishes into the sink with a crash. A couple of the plates broke and she grimaced. The front door slammed suddenly and she hurried into the family room to peer out the window. She watched as Ellery backed out of the driveway and sped off down the road toward town.

A choice expletive slipped from her lips. She

snatched his empty plate from the coffee table. After cleaning up the glass in the sink and loading the dishwasher, she checked on Clarissa, who was sitting on her bed, a pair of earbuds tightly plugged into her ears.

Thankful that her daughter was safe and sound, she went back downstairs, prepared to wait Ellery out. There was no way she was going to stand for this anymore. Grail land or no Grail land, vineyard or no vineyard, she wanted a divorce.

Admitting the realization to herself lifted a huge weight off her shoulders. She'd been pretending for so long…

And for what?

Yes, this vineyard had been her home. It was really all she knew. But holding onto it had become hell. It had been hell for years now. She knew she had no choice but to let it go.

She walked into the kitchen and pulled a bottle of wine from the chiller. After pouring herself a glass, she went into the family room and sat down on the couch. She turned off the lights and watched, her eyes staring into the darkness that was just taking over outside.

Hour after hour went by. The bottle of wine disappeared. Anne Marie found herself drifting off. When she woke up, sun was coming through the front window. She realized she'd fallen asleep on the couch. A little frantically, she got to her feet. She peered out at the driveway, expecting to see Ellery's Lincoln parked next to her BMW. It wasn't there. Ellery hadn't come home the night before.

. . .

Jarett was just about to wake up Alex for breakfast when he heard frantic pounding on the front door. He glanced at the watch on his wrist. It read six-thirty AM. Who the hell was so annoying at this hour?

When he opened the door, he found his sister-in-law standing there. *Naturally*, he thought to himself.

Anne Marie was nearly unrecognizable. Her hair, which was normally perfectly shellacked with hair spray, was sticking out in different directions. Her clothing was rumpled as if she'd slept in it. Even her makeup was smeared and looked like hell.

He frowned at her. "What happened to you?" He was a little worried she'd been attacked again.

"Is Ellery here?" She came right in, nearly stepping on his stocking feet in the process. She moved from room to room, her eyes scanning every nook and cranny.

"No, he's not here. What is wrong with

you?"

She finally turned and met his gaze. "He didn't come home last night."

"Oh." He stood there dumbly for a minute. "Did you check the cellar?"

"I checked the cellar, the vineyard. Everywhere! Why do you think I look like this?"

He narrowed his eyes. She was coming apart at the seams, right before his eyes. "Calm down."

"I will not calm down! I'm done with this! I can't take it anymore!" She crumbled abruptly into a fit of tears.

Jarett was so shocked he didn't know what to say or do. Anne Marie just wasn't a crier. A screamer? Yes. A seether, grumbler, snapper—even a hisser—but not a crier. Not unless something was really wrong.

"You should sit down," he eventually said, taking her arm and leading her toward the family room.

Sniveling, she sat down on the couch and rubbed at her already splotchy face.

He folded his arms over his chest and waited for her to settle down.

"He's a bastard. You can say what you want about me, but he's the one who's killing this marriage."

Not this again. He wanted to sigh but he didn't. "What happened?"

"Like I said, he didn't come home last night. And he was gone all day yesterday, too."

Jarett hadn't been working on the vineyard for the last couple of days. He'd been home, keeping an eye on Alex. He had no idea where Ellery had been spending his time. He didn't say as much to Anne Marie. "He was probably in a meeting or something."

"There were no meetings on his schedule. And don't you dare lie for him!" She glared fiercely. "You don't even like him!"

He couldn't really argue with that. He thought his next words over carefully. Eventually he gave up on sparing her feelings. "I don't know what you want me to say, Anne Marie. Ellery is Ellery. He's your husband. You're choosing to stay married to him." He felt a little hypocritical. He'd said the same words to Ellery weeks earlier about her.

"Don't think I don't know you're on his side," she snapped, wiping at her eyes with the sleeve of her silk blouse. When she saw the black mascara stain on the material, she crumbled again. "Damn it, I'm a mess! A complete, freaking mess!"

"There may be a rational explanation for his absence. Have you tried calling him?"

"Yes, multiple times. He's not answering. He did the same thing to me yesterday." She sniffled but refrained from wiping her nose on her shirt this time. "He's with another woman. That's the only explanation."

Jarett had to admit things seemed suspicious.

"Why don't you try calling him?"

"What makes you think he'll answer me?"

"It's different when you call. You're not his wife. When you call it's for a serious reason, not just to ask him where he is."

He supposed she was right about that. And she was calming down a little. He didn't want to give her a reason to get started on the waterworks again. He dug his phone from his pocket and hit his brother's number. The phone rang a number of times before he was sent to voicemail. At the beep, he left a message. "Ellery, it's Jarett. Call me as soon as you get this message. It's important." He hung up.

Anne Marie continued to sit there sniffling. Jarett, unsure what to do, gestured toward the kitchen. "Do you want some coffee? He might call back in the meantime if you wait long enough." He really didn't want her hanging around but he didn't see any way around that. He didn't want to send her back to Clarissa the way she was.

Smoothing her hair down, she stood up.

"Can I use your bathroom first? I don't want anyone else to see me this way."

"You know where it is."

He went into the kitchen, prepared to make some coffee. He found Alex standing near the breakfast bar, fully dressed, a curious expression on her face.

"I didn't know you were up."

"I heard the pounding on the door. I thought it might be Jack."

"No such luck." He got the coffee pot going.

"What's happening?"

"Ellery didn't come home last night."

She waited for him to say more.

"Don't ask me to understand the craziness. Apparently ping pong cheating is still unexpected."

"He's cheating again?"

He turned, leaning against the countertop. "Well he didn't come home. I doubt if he stayed at the inn."

She blew out a breath just as Anne Marie came into the room. She'd obviously washed her face. Her makeup was gone. Her hair had been tamed significantly and she'd already gone to work scrubbing the stain off the sleeve of her blouse.

"I'm sorry I bothered you so early." Her gaze moved to Alex. "If I woke you, I apologize."

"I was awake," Alex replied.

Jarett poured Anne Marie some coffee and offered the mug to her.

She accepted it cautiously.

He poured a cup for himself. Alex went for a bottle of juice. Then an uncomfortable silence overtook the room.

Luckily, his phone rang. Anne Marie glanced toward the ID hopefully. It wasn't Ellery calling. It was Clem. He knew the guys were on the job at the resort already. He gave Alex and apologetic glance. "It's Clem. I'd better take it." He stepped out of the room.

. . .

Alex had no idea what to say to Anne Marie and it was obvious that Anne Marie had no idea what to say to Alex, either.

Eventually, Alex gestured to the breakfast bar. "If you're hungry I can make something."

"Don't pretend to be nice. It's irritating," Anne Marie said solemnly.

Alex arched a brow. "Okay, what would you like me to do? Kick you in the ass?"

Anne Marie's lips quirked, surprising Alex a little. "No, I'm not in the mood to spar. Besides, you shouldn't get violent in your condition."

Alex grunted at that. She took a stool and sat. "You might as well sit down if you're planning to stay for the time being. It annoys me when people hover around uncomfortably."

"Touché," Anne Marie said, and sat. She stared into her coffee cup. "I'm sure you're getting a big kick out of all this."

"Out of what?" Alex asked.

"The fact that my marriage is a mess."

Alex fiddled with her juice bottle, making no move to open it. "Unlike some people, I don't get joy out of other people's misfortunes."

"Don't you? You let your aunt come to work at my gift shop."

"That was Jarett, not me. I told him it was a bad idea."

"And look how it turned out."

"Like I said, not my idea."

Anne Marie set her coffee cup down and rested her head in her hands. "I have no freaking clue how I've gotten to this point in my life."

A little startled, Alex rested her elbows on the counter. "I've taken a few interesting turns in life myself."

Anne Marie snorted. Then she shook her head. "I would have done anything for him. Literally. I had it in my head that if I just convinced you to sell—that if I could just get

207

my hands on your property, everything with Ellery and me—it would magically work itself out."

"Why? Because then you could screw Jarett out of his share of the vineyard?"

Anne Marie shrugged and nodded. Then she let out a sigh. "That was the plan. Unfortunately, I've finally realized that no matter what I do, Jarett will always be one step ahead of me. He's too well protected financially for me to ever overtake him. He'll always have the upper hand."

"He's a smart guy," Alex admitted with pride.

"Yeah, I think I married the wrong brother." Anne Marie took another sip of coffee. Then she surprised Alex by looking her in the eye. "I didn't think you had it in you. To stay, to stick this out. I have to say, I underestimated you, too."

Alex wasn't sure how to respond to the revelation.

"I won't get in your way around here anymore, just so you know. I can see you and Jarett are the real deal. As painful as I find that, I know when to throw in the towel. I'm going to ask Ellery for a divorce."

"What does one thing have to do with the other?" Alex wanted to know.

"I think you're smart enough to figure out that Ellery and I should have divorced years ago. The vineyard is the only thing holding us together. Even our daughter isn't enough to do that. It's always been about the money. And it's mostly been me. Ellery couldn't give less of a damn about this place."

Alex took a sip of juice. She found herself feeling a little bit sorry for Anne Marie, despite the fact that she'd made her own bed.

"I don't expect sympathy. I know how you feel about me—how Jarett feels." She set her empty coffee cup aside. "It is what it is." She stood.

"Aren't you going to stick around and see if Ellery calls back?" Alex stood, too.

"No. I'm going to go home, start sorting things out in my life, and figure out what comes next."

Alex had to hand it to Anne Marie. She was finally doing something commendable. She walked her to the door and shut it behind her once she'd left.

"You handled that amazingly well."

She turned, met Jarett's gaze. He was standing in the hallway outside the kitchen, a guilty grin on his face. "How long have you been standing there?"

"Long enough. I've never heard her talk like

that. It actually sounded like she has a...*heart.*"

He feigned a shocked expression and she found herself grinning. "She does, Jarett. And right now, I think it's broken."

"If he is cheating, it's in retaliation—not that that's okay."

"Maybe. But I think her heart's broken more because she failed her parents. She knows what's going to happen when she walks away from Ellery."

He didn't seem all that sympathetic. "I hate to change the subject but we've got a problem out at the resort. Clem called. He's over at the cabin by the lake, mowing. There's a waterline issue out there. He thinks the whole cabin might be flooded but he can't get in. He needs the key."

"I can take it to him. I know you have work to do."

"We'll both go. I'm not sending you anywhere near that place by yourself again. Especially in a car."

19

CeCe glared at Jack's television set. She had a choice of the late afternoon news, various different talk shows or reruns of *Roseanne*. She chose the reruns.

Glancing at her watch, she realized it was after three. Jack had gone off to check in at the office just after one. He'd promised to be back before dinner. Time was crawling by. She was stuck on the couch—direct orders from the doctor at the hospital. She was bored as hell and irritable. And she was starting to get hungry.

Wishing for a pile of her famous fries, she got off the couch and headed into the kitchen. She dug through Jack's refrigerator, which consisted of beer, cheese and cold cuts.

She frowned. If she was going to be hanging around his place more often, she was going to have to get herself some staples.

A knock on the front door sounded and she grimaced. Had Jack forgotten his keys?

She crossed the room and peered through the peephole. She didn't see anyone there. Changing her vantage point, she peeked through the front window. She saw a newspaper lying on the porch. Obviously when the paperboy had tossed it, he'd hit the door, thus resulting in the knock she'd heard.

She opened the door and went after the paper, figuring it was something better to observe than the boring television.

She realized pretty quickly she was in trouble. A hand came out of nowhere and shoved her into the house. Before she could take a breath, her nose was overcome with a pungent chemical smell. Her vision blurred. Her eyes grew heavy. She tried to fight back but her limbs became useless almost immediately. She hit the floor in a stupor an instant later.

· · ·

Mercy took a long look around the guesthouse. She'd cleaned every nook and cranny. She'd packed up her things—Evie's things. She hadn't told her daughter yet, but the car was all loaded. They were going to move on to greener pastures. She'd called her ex in Seattle. As much as she hated the sonofabitch, he was helping her out by finding her a place to stay. He was going to take care of Evie until she found a job and got back on her feet.

Mercy knew it was the right thing to do for Evie's sake. She deserved a right to know her father, even if he was a cheating bastard.

All she needed to do now was head up to the main house and get Evie into the car. That was going to be the hardest part of all this. School had started a couple of weeks earlier and she knew Evie liked her friends. She also knew how close her daughter was to Clarissa. Even though the girls had been somewhat toxic together at times, she suspected their close relationship had saved them both from completely self-destructing.

Taking one last glance around, she grabbed the spare key and locked the front door. Then she turned and headed across the grass.

About halfway there, she got a very strange feeling. It was broad daylight. There was no reason for her to be on edge.

Yet she was. Instinctively she knew someone was following her. She reached for the weapon she'd been carrying recently and realized it was in her purse in her packed vehicle.

Turning, her eyes scanned the grassy field. There was nobody behind her. Everything was quiet. Peaceful.

Deserted.

She knew the security detail did rounds regularly. Perhaps they were on the other side of the vineyard.

She pulled her coat tighter around herself. Just as she was about to pivot in the other direction, she felt someone come up behind her. A hand came around and she instantly smelled a strong chemical. She tried to fight, but it was no use. The ground whooshed up and slapped her into darkness.

. . .

Anne Marie lifted her phone and scrolled through to Ellery's number. For the fifth time that day, she hit connect. She hadn't left a message so far. This time she was going to. If he didn't want to talk to her face to face, she was going to get her point across another way. There was no way in hell she was letting him back into the house.

The phone sent her to voicemail. She stepped out onto the front porch, careful to make sure Clarissa, who was upstairs with Evie doing her homework, didn't hear her.

At the beep, she unleashed her wrath. "You listen, you selfish bastard. This is over. Do you understand me? *Finished.* You told me the other day that I need to decide when I don't need this vineyard to legitimize me anymore. Well, that time is now, Ellery. Even more, I don't need *you* to make me feel legitimate. I've already spoken to Spenser Malin so don't bother contacting him. I've also spoken to your brother. In other words, you can just go to hell." She disconnected the call, feeling significantly better.

She turned to go back into the house. She didn't even make it to the front door. A black cloth came at her face with brutal force. She smelled the chemical, choked on it for a moment as she tried to scream for help. She knew there were two security guards patrolling the backside of the vineyard. She'd seen them earlier that day multiple times.

Her brain began to shut down and she felt her phone drop to the front porch with a clatter. That was the last sound she heard before she lost consciousness.

• • •

Jarett steered the truck down the gritty road toward the cabin by the lake. He'd had to field a couple of business calls before they'd left so the sun was beginning to go down by this point.

Alex sat next to him, taking in the scenery.

When they reached the turn off for the cabin, he pulled into the parking area. He saw Clem's truck was there. Everything seemed quiet. There was a mower out in front of the cabin, sitting motionless.

The hairs on the back of his neck stood on end and he glanced at Alex. She was staring out the window, a tense expression on her own face.

"What?" he asked.

"I thought you said they were mowing." She lifted up the key and offered it to him. "Where is everyone?"

"Roger went home sick earlier. As for Clem, I don't know. Around back maybe. Stay here while I go check it out."

"I don't' want to stay here."

He shot a hostile stare her way and flipped open the glovebox. *"Stay here.* If anything happens and I don't come back right away, this is here. Do you know how to use it?" He lifted the paperwork for his vehicle so she could see the 9mm handgun that was stowed underneath.

"Yes, I know how to use it. But what about

you?"

"I don't need a gun to protect myself. Just sit tight and wait until I come back."

"Jarett—" she began, reaching for him.

"It'll be okay, Alex. Clem's probably out back or something. Just in case…" He gestured to the glovebox.

She let go of his arm reluctantly.

He stepped out of the vehicle, leaving the keys inside with her as he locked it.

During his time in the military, he'd learned to rely on his instincts. Right at that moment, those instincts were kicking in full force. He knew something here wasn't right.

He strode down the incline cautiously until he could get a look inside the guest cabin. The first thing he noticed was that the window was broken.

The second thing he noticed was that there was no water anywhere—no sign of a water line problem.

A sick feeling began to pool in the pit of his stomach.

"I want you to come quietly. Real quietly. If you don't, I'll go get her first and she'll pay the price for your stupidity."

He turned around slowly, prepared to do battle.

Clem Taylor stood behind him, a small

caliber handgun in his grip. It was pointed straight at Jarett's chest.

Jarett's hands gradually raised. "What's this about, Clem?"

"Haven't you figured it out yet?"

"Figured *what* out?"

Clem's eyes darkened. "You people really are stupid as hell, aren't you?" He gestured for Jarett to follow him. "I mean it. One wrong move and I'll take it out on your girl. Pregnant or not, I could give a shit about her."

Jarett started to sweat. He knew he could take Clem down, gun or not. What worried him was what wasn't right in front of him. He had a very strong feeling that Clem wasn't here alone.

Clem turned and moved toward the door to the cabin. Jarett had no choice but to follow.

"Get her out of that truck and get over here!" Clem called over his shoulder.

Jarett turned, alarmed. That's when he saw *her.* A young woman with long, curly blond hair, a dark, angry shadow over her eyes. She stepped into the clearing and approached Jarett's truck so quickly he had no alternative but to yell to get Alex's attention. Before he could do much more than that, the butt of Clem's gun slammed into the back of his head. He felt himself falling. He struggled to hold onto consciousness but it was no use. His body hit the ground and he was out.

20

Alex heard Jarett's warning. She reached for the glovebox just as something crashed through the passenger side window of the truck, shattering glass everywhere. She ducked instinctively, covering her head with her hands.

"Get out of the truck!"

She heard the female voice, winced at the commanding tone to it. When she lifted her head, she found herself staring into a familiar pair of eyes. Eyes that looked very much like those of Erica Haynes. Her face was older, more mature. Her blond hair was the same as it had been years ago—even the curls.

The memories came floating back like they'd happened yesterday. Alex remembered playing in the campground with this girl, swimming at the lake. She remembered the last time she'd seen Erica—that horrible scream as she'd fallen from the treehouse.

"I said, get out of the truck!" The door suddenly whipped open. Alex felt fingers grip her arm. She managed to land on her feet as she hit the ground. True terror slapped her viciously when she turned and saw Jarett face down in the dirt just outside the cabin.

"What did you do?" she cried, getting a little hysterical.

"Move!" She was poked in the back brutally with a gun. She had no choice but to move forward.

When they reached the front stoop, she attempted to lean over and check on Jarett. A jab to her back sent her flailing over the top of him and through the open front door.

She smelled mildew immediately and it made her stomach roll. The cabin was dark except for what was left of the early evening sunlight.

Alex was surprised to realize she wasn't alone. She recognized Clem Taylor first. He was standing directly in front of her, a gun in his hand. She started to shake her head in denial.

"Join your friends. Everything will be crystal

clear here in a minute." Clem gave her a shove and she stumbled across the room.

Anne Marie was huddled in one corner, her eyes bleary as she stared up at Alex helplessly. Next to her was Mercy, terrified and shaking. CeCe completed the group. She was still out cold.

"Sit!" Alex was shoved to the ground roughly by Clem.

"Why are you doing this?" She stared at him, completely baffled.

"Think about it, Alex. Think real, real hard."

Erica stepped up, her eyes full of venomous anger. "One for all and all for one. Protect each other 'til day is done. Is that the right oath?" She stared from woman to woman.

Mercy whimpered. Anne Marie stayed silent. CeCe opened her eyes slowly and recoiled when she saw what was happening.

"Seems a little more frightening when you're the ones being ridiculed, doesn't it?" Clem gave Alex a saccharine smile. "You're all a bunch of liars. Every one of you."

"I told the truth," Alex said quietly. "I never lied about what happened."

"*They* did." He gestured to Anne Marie and Mercy. "I ought to kill them both right now. The world doesn't need trash like them around." He took a threatening step toward

Anne Marie and Mercy. They both started screaming.

"You listen to me, you little bitch!" Clem grabbed Anne Marie by the arm and hauled her to her feet. Again, Anne Marie let out a shriek. "Shut up!" He shook her violently. "Do you hear me? You don't get to cry in front of me! My sister didn't get that chance!"

Alex took the words in and digested them.

My sister.

She held herself deathly still as she studied Clem closely. It took her a while but she finally caught it.

The resemblance.

"Buddy." She spoke quietly and he turned away from Anne Marie's screaming and locked eyes with hers. He let Anne Marie go abruptly. She scampered back into the corner and cowered with Mercy.

"My real name is Clemson, but yes, I used to go by Buddy. My middle name is Taylor. I'm surprised you remember."

"I remember." She straightened.

Sweat was popping out on his brow now. "Do you remember my sister?"

"Of course I do. Do you think I could ever forget that night?" She stared over his shoulder at Erica, who was standing near the doorway. "I'm sorry. For whatever you went through."

Clem's eyes narrowed and he started to laugh. "This is sweet. Really, really sweet." He yanked Alex by the arm this time. He hauled her closer to his sister, to the point where they were nearly in each other's faces. "Take a real hard look."

Alex told herself not to panic. She did every exercise she could think of to keep herself from falling apart. She had to stay strong. If not for herself, for her baby.

"Look!" Clem screamed again.

She lifted her head and stared into Erica's eyes a second time. Now that they were so close, she could see something was different. No exercise in the world could have prepared her for what she saw.

Blue. The woman's eyes were *blue.*

Erica's eyes hadn't been. They'd been big and round and *brown.*

Alex shuddered. This woman wasn't Erica Haynes after all. But she definitely looked a lot like her.

"I think she's finally figured it out, Clem."

"I think she has, too." Clem tightened his grip on Alex's arm. "Meet my other sister, Willa."

Alex was stunned into silence. When the Haynes family had been in Mystery Lake twenty years earlier, there'd been no Willa

Haynes. Obviously, Paul and Carolyn Haynes had welcomed another daughter after they'd left town. And she was the spitting image of her older sister.

"Where is Erica?" Clem demanded angrily.

Alex started to shake her head.

"Don't you dare go into denial! We're past all that! I want to know where my sister is!"

"I don't know!" she eventually yelled back.

"One of you does!" He shoved Alex to the ground again. "We're going to sit here all night until that person finally tells the truth. Do you understand me?"

"None of us know!" CeCe exclaimed, suddenly coming alive. "Erica fell from the treehouse and then she disappeared!"

"She's somewhere," Clem insisted, lowering his voice. "Nobody just evaporates. Isn't that right, Alex?" He smirked in Alex's direction. "I have to tell you, I'm sorry you had to find out about your mother the way you did. When I found her—left her on your porch—I was trying to remind you of Erica. I didn't know who those bones really belonged to. I thought they were my sister's."

So Clem had been the one to put the bones on Mimi's porch. Alex bit back a wave of nausea. "You *found* her?"

"Yes, I found her. I've been here for over a

225

year, you know. Watching. Following each of you at different times."

The idea was chilling and Alex shivered.

He peered over at CeCe. "Erica liked you. She told me all about you." He turned back to Alex. "And you. She was so excited to learn that cadence. She really wanted to be a member of your stupid, little club. She practiced for hours. I remember yelling at her for driving me nuts with the knocking." He snorted. "And that stupid oath…"

"I liked Erica," Alex said honestly. "Nobody meant for her to get hurt. It was a terrible accident."

"Trust me, the police told us all about the *accident*. You two were the worst." He directed this toward Anne Marie and Mercy. "You've lied, time and time again. You didn't care if Erica was ever found, did you? It doesn't matter to you even now." He shook his head, his expression full of disgust and sorrow. "Losing Erica literally broke my mother's heart. Her dying wish was for her daughter to be buried properly."

"It matters to me," Mercy argued solemnly.

"Sure, it does." He turned his wrath on Anne Marie a second time. "You make me sick. You and that fucked up husband of yours."

Anne Marie recoiled again.

Clem glanced over his shoulder. "He still out?"

Willa perused the doorway where Alex saw that Jarett was still lying motionless. There was a trail of blood dribbling down the side of his head. He didn't look like he was breathing at all.

"He's out," Willa confirmed.

"Go get the others."

Confused, Alex watched as Willa walked to the bathroom door and opened it. She disappeared inside. When she returned, she was pushing Ellery, her gun at his back. There was a smattering of dried blood on the side of his face and he looked like he'd been through a war zone. He was shoved into a sitting position not far from Anne Marie and Mercy, who gasped.

Willa went back into the bathroom. This time when she came out, Alex was completely stunned. Gypsy was in tow, her hands tied in front of her. Her face was a mess of bruises and there was a cut above her left eye. She met Alex's gaze immediately. "Well shit, honey pie. This is not how I planned on spending my time here in Mystery Lake."

"Keep quiet. I've heard enough from you," Clem seethed. He grabbed Gypsy by the arm and shoved her in the opposite direction. "Grab the tape in case we have to shut her up again," he instructed his sister.

Willa went for a roll of duct tape that was resting on the kitchen table.

"If you'd let me say something, you might get the freaking answers you're looking for." Gypsy got to her knees, struggling to slide her ropes off.

"You didn't shut up all night last night," Clem growled at her.

"That's because you taped my mouth shut!" Gypsy's expression darkened. "And you locked me up with that prick!" She glared over at Ellery. "It's *him* you want. Not them. He's the one who killed your sister. He killed my sister, too."

Ellery was moving suddenly, across the room toward Gypsy. "Shut up! You're nothing but a whore! A worthless, teasing whore!"

"Oh my God," Alex heard Anne Marie exclaim.

"You move one more inch and I'm going to do the world a *real* favor," Clem threatened, giving Ellery a good kick to the ribs.

Ellery rolled over with an oomph.

"He thinks I'm Leona," Gypsy went on, before anyone could stop her. "He's had me locked up for the past two days. I've tried to get through to him—tried to tell him who I really am. He's just not listening." She scowled up at Clem. "And then this Neanderthal came after us—"

"Shut up, Gypsy," Alex interrupted, seeing that Clem was close to coming undone.

Gypsy shook her head. "You all need to listen to me. Ellery Rhodes is crazy. He kept telling me I was supposed to be dead. Then he kept apologizing to me. He's the one who killed Leona. And she was just the beginning."

Alex narrowed her eyes. "What are you talking about?"

"He was having an affair with her—with Leona. When she refused to leave her husband, her daughter—" Gypsy shot an apologetic look in Alex's direction, "—he killed her."

The words echoed inside Alex's head.

"You're lying!" Anne Marie accused.

"Sorry, sweetie. I'm not. Your husband is not a nice guy." Gypsy's voice didn't hold an ounce of sympathy.

"She loved me!" Ellery cried, before Anne Marie could say anything. "Leona loved me and we were going to be together!"

Alex refused to believe any of this was true. Her mother had been thirty years old. Ellery had been sixteen—a teenager! It just wasn't possible...

Gypsy spoke directly to Clem. "Your sister

saw the whole thing. She was injured, running through the woods. She was trying to get cell service. She had a phone but it wouldn't work. It was broken."

"She's lying," Ellery moaned. "She's a fucking liar!"

Clem gave Ellery another brutal kick, then turned back to Gypsy and waited for her to say more.

Gypsy was only too happy to oblige. "He told me Erica saw him hit Leona in the back of the head with a rock. He went after her once he realized. She already had a broken arm. She was bleeding. She promised she wouldn't tell but he didn't believe her. He killed her anyway."

Alex saw Clem flinch and shake his head. He rubbed a hand over his jaw and stared up at the ceiling for a moment. "I've been on that bastard's tail for months now. I saw him placing flowers up in the hills one day. After he left, I dug. I found those bones. I thought they were Erica's. The phone was buried there with them. I put two and two together—I remembered the police mentioning a missing cell phone. I was so angry. I was angry at him, at you." He glared at Alex. "At all of you!"

"You should have taken the bones to the police," Alex said solemnly.

A tear rolled down his cheek. "I wasn't ready to tell anyone who I really was at that point. I was still looking for answers—still trying to figure out what happened that night."

"So you put the bones up in the treehouse," Alex guessed.

He nodded soberly. "Eventually, I put them there for safekeeping. I needed to figure out what to do with them. I didn't realize anyone ever went up there. When those girls found them…" He raked a hand through his hair. "I felt bad about that. I knew I needed to get them to the police. I couldn't just outright hand them over so I left them on your porch. When it turned out they weren't Erica's, I didn't know what to think."

"It was you that sent those letters—you that left the phone for Anne Marie," Alex figured out. "You're responsible for the attacks, the cadence. Everything." And Willa had obviously been the woman they had mistaken for Erica.

"Let me get something straight here," he began. "I didn't intend to hurt anyone. Things got out of hand. All I've ever wanted was justice for my sister. She was twelve years old. She mattered to me. She mattered to my family. But she didn't matter to any of you."

"That's not true," Alex argued.

"It *is* true! That's why I had to take matters

into my own hands. I caused some problems at the vineyard—a little vandalism here and there—trying to jar a few memories, but nothing fazed anyone." He kept his eyes on Alex. "Not until your grandmother died and you came home. That's when I knew I had to step up my game."

Alex told herself not to react to the words.

"You're the one who vandalized the vineyard?" Anne Marie asked thickly, sitting up straight.

"I didn't do anything too terrible. A few derogatory words here and there with some spray paint. A small fire." Clem shrugged unapologetically. "If you'd been paying attention, things wouldn't have gone as far as they have."

Anne Marie's eyes darkened. "*You* set that fire."

"Your daughter was the perfect scapegoat." Clem didn't even blink.

Anne Marie's whole face changed. Her blue eyes turned to ice. "You sonofabitch."

Unmoved, he turned away from her.

"You cut the brake lines in my car, didn't you?" Furious in her own right, Alex glared up at him. "You could have killed me. How would that have gotten you any answers for your sister?"

He narrowed his eyes and shook his head. "Now wait a minute. I'm responsible for the other things—the vandalism, the fire. I left those letters and the phone, those bones. I did some prowling at night that went a little too far. But I didn't cut any brake lines. There's no way I'm going to go down for that. That's attempted murder."

She didn't believe him for a minute. She sensed that pushing him would be a mistake so she closed her mouth.

He scratched at his chin and scowled down at Ellery. "If you buried her mother and the phone my sister had—if you killed them both, you know where Erica is."

Ellery groaned and rolled over.

Clem gave him another violent kick to the ribs. "Where the fuck is my sister?"

Ellery still refused to speak.

"Tell him, Ellery."

Alex lifted her head and glanced toward the doorway. She felt instant relief when she realized Jarett was alive and well, standing on the porch, his gun in his hands. It was pointed in Clem's direction. He shook his head at Willa when she attempted to turn toward him with her weapon.

She lowered her gun, defeated.

"No," Ellery said, starting to whimper. "No,

I don't know!"

"You do." Jarett kept his eyes on Clem, but he spoke to his brother in a low tone. "Make this right. Give Erica back to her family."

Ellery stared up at Jarett imploringly. "Just kill me. I don't care anymore. Kill me, please!"

"Don't you dare kill him until he tells us where Erica is!" Clem warned, finally losing it all together. "Tell me!" He gave Ellery another vicious kick. "Tell me where she is!"

"I loved her! I loved Leona!" Ellery wailed pathetically. "She told me she was going to leave her family—that we were going to be together! But she was cheating! I caught her with Ben Haggerty—with other men! Damn her!" Ellery dissolved into a fit of tears. He sounded completely delusional, yet some of what he said put other things that had happened into perspective—specifically, Ben Haggerty's resentment toward Alex and her family.

Sirens were coming up the lane suddenly. Apparently Jarett had managed to call for help when he'd retrieved his gun. The cabin was swarming with cops seconds later.

Jarett was in front of Alex instantly, pulling her to her feet. "Are you okay? Are you hurt anywhere?"

"I'm okay," she assured him, holding onto

his arms and trying to get a grip on reality. She was still reeling from everything she'd heard.

"He's a rotten apple, that one," Gypsy said, once she'd been untied. "He showed up at your house and ransacked the place. He had a gun. He threatened to kill me a dozen times, in all kinds of horrible ways. He wanted that will—all your financial statements. He was determined to find a way to get that land from you. When he came up empty…" She shivered. "He dragged me out of that house, suitcase and all, kicking and screaming. He swore we were finally going to be together. It was like a light switch flipped and suddenly I was my sister."

The words sickened Alex. "Are you okay?"

"He didn't really hurt me. I can take care of myself."

Gypsy's bruised face said otherwise but Alex didn't bother pointing that out.

Clem and Willa were cuffed by two of Jack's deputies and led from the cabin.

Mercy and Anne Marie were huddled together again. Mercy was providing as much support as she could. Anne Marie was definitely beyond upset, not that Alex could blame her.

CeCe made a beeline for Jack, who greeted her with open arms.

Ellery continued to lie in a heap, bawling his

head off. Two other deputies were doing their best to get him in cuffs. The sight of him was sickening.

"I know you've had to swallow a lot at this point, honey pie," Gypsy began again. "But you should know, Ellery's the one who tampered with your car. He told me that, too. He was willing to do just about anything to get rid of you—to get you out of the way so he could get your land."

Alex saw Jarett's jaw go rigid. Before she could stop him, he stepped forward and landed his own swift kick to Ellery's back. He leaned over and spoke in his brother's ear. "Rot in hell, you sonofabitch."

He ignored the wail Ellery let out. He straightened, set his arm around Alex's shoulders, and led her, along with Gypsy, outside. They could still hear Ellery screaming as they climbed into Jarett's truck and drove away.

EPILOGUE

One year later…

Alex watched her four-month-old son sleep, his tiny fingers balled up as he lay on his back in his crib.

Brayden Jarett Rhodes had come into the world three months earlier, red faced and screaming. Jarett had been the first to hold him. Alex had been the second. Gypsy had been the third.

The baby had turned all their lives upside down since his arrival. And Alex had loved every minute of it.

The past year had been a trial. Ellery had confessed to killing both Leona and Erica. He'd finally led the authorities to Erica's remains. She'd been up on the hill behind the resort for the last twenty years, not far from where Leona had been buried. She was now back in Montana, at rest near her mother. Leona, too, had been given a proper burial in the town cemetery.

Her mother had lacked morals, that was obvious. Still, Alex had felt the need to give her an appropriate resting place.

Both Willa and Clem (Buddy) Haynes had been charged with a variety of crimes. They had ended up fighting their way through the court system. Willa got a slap on the wrist, due to the fact that she was barely eighteen. Clem's situation had been a bit more complicated. Luckily for both of them, their father was a criminal lawyer.

The mystery of Butch's death had been solved. Ellery eventually claimed responsibility for that, as well. He and Butch, after years of animosity, had faced off in the woods the night of the treehouse fire. Butch had lost that battle, much the same way as Leona and Erica had.

For years, Alex had longed for the answers to so many questions that haunted her and finally, now she had them. A huge weight had been lifted off of her.

"He asleep?"

Alex glanced over her shoulder. "He's out."

Jarett crept into the room and stood behind her, staring down at his son proudly. He wrapped his arms around her from behind. "Maybe he'll sleep through the night tonight."

"I doubt it," she said, smiling. Brayden did his best screaming in the middle of the night while they were trying to sleep.

They both tiptoed out of the nursery. "So how did things go?" She spoke once they were out of Brayden's earshot.

"It's done. Papers are signed. The vineyard's Anne Marie's again." He gave her a skeptical look. "Hopefully she takes the advice of the efficiency expert I referred her to. Otherwise, she's going to be right back where she was when I bailed her out the first time."

"It's nice what you did."

"Giving her back her inheritance?" He shrugged. "It was the right thing to do. I made a good profit off the buy back."

She arched a brow. She knew for a fact he'd taken care of Anne Marie and Clarissa without making one penny of profit. He'd been lucky to break even.

"It was the right thing to do," he repeated. "With Ellery in prison for good…" His voice trailed off. "I wasn't about to let them go under. They've both been through enough."

Alex knew he felt bad about what his brother had done. The betrayal was hanging over everyone in Ellery's family. The healing process was a long one that she knew wasn't going to happen overnight, but at least it had begun.

"I talked to Mercy today," she said, changing the subject. "She's all settled back in Seattle. I guess things with Ralph are looking up." Mercy had recently reconciled with her ex-husband. Alex wasn't sure she cared for the cocky attorney all that much but Mercy claimed she was head over heels again. She was convinced Ralph had changed. Evie was happy. Hopefully things would work out for the best for all of them.

"Jack called. He and CeCe are on their way to Bermuda. You're supposed to water her plants," he reminded her.

Jack and CeCe had gotten married a week earlier. They were currently on their honeymoon. It had taken them a good year, but they'd managed to pull their relationship together and make it permanent. They were both happy and planning to search for a house as soon as they got back from their trip.

"Hello? Where are you two?"

Alex stiffened at the sound of Gypsy's voice coming from downstairs.

Jarett grimaced. "She has a nasty habit of coming right in without knocking."

"Yes," Alex agreed. "She does."

Gypsy had been staying at the resort in Mimi's old house and helping them run the business. Jarett and Alex were still living in his house on the vineyard. It was the one thing on the property he'd refused to sign over to Anne Marie.

Heading downstairs, they met Gypsy in the foyer. "We've got a full campground, honey pies. Even the cabin by the lake is rented. I can't wait until construction on the others is complete."

The cabin by the lake had been remodeled. Alex had put some of CeCe's ideas to use and added a private hot tub, firepit and a full kitchen and bedroom. Eight other cabins were currently under construction.

"That's good," Jarett remarked, eyeing the bags in Gypsy's arms with curiosity. "I thought we talked about the toy thing. You're spoiling the kid."

"I'm his great-auntie. That's my prerogative. Besides, these aren't from me. The parents sent them. Remember, they're coming in for a visit in a couple of weeks. You two had better be bracing yourselves."

Alex had met her grandparents multiple

times now. The relationship was new, but they were all working on getting over the past.

"Well, I need to get back. I'll just leave these here. Time for my rounds." Gypsy took her evening rounds at the campground very seriously. She had her own golf cart and she loved meeting everyone that came to stay.

When she was gone, Jarett made a face at the packages she'd left behind. "Between your family and my family, we're not going to have room for any of our own stuff."

She grinned. "They mean well. He's a baby. When he grows up that will change."

"Yeah, then they'll start showering him with money like they do Clarissa." He wrapped his arms around her, pulling her into his embrace. "Have I told you lately how happy you make me? Everything I want is right here in this house. I truly love you, Alexa Rhodes."

She was still getting used to hearing her name attached to his. They'd only been married for a few months.

"I love you, too," she whispered back, lifting her head toward his. Finally, after a lifetime of running away, she had the family she'd always wanted and a place she truly could call home.

For more information follow
Jennifer Hayden-Author on Facebook.

AVAILABLE TITLES BY JENNIFER HAYDEN

HIDE AND SEEK
(Book 1 Hide and Seek Mystery Series)
UNBROKEN
(Book 2 Hide and Seek Mystery Series)
COLLISION
(Book 3 Hide and Seek Mystery Series)
SWEET REVENGE
SAY MERCY
SOUNDS OF NIGHT
ROOT OF ALL EVIL
AFTER THE RAIN
(Book 1 – The Callahans)
IN THE EYE OF THE STORM
(Book 2 – The Callahans)
AFTERSHOCK
(Book 3 – The Callahans)
LESS THAN PERFECT
(Book 4 - The Callahans)
DESERT HEAT
(Book 5 – The Callahans)
SHATTERED
(Book 6 – The Callahans)
HOPE FOR CHRISTMAS

SPEAK NO EVIL
(Book 1 in Noel, Montana)
HEAD OVER HEELS FOR CHRISTMAS
(Book 2 in Noel, Montana)
SKELETONS IN THE MIST
(The McCalls – Book 1)
BENEATH BURIED SECRETS
(The McCalls – Book 2)
FATAL VOWS
(The McCalls – Book 3)
HIDDEN MEMORIES
SHAMELESS
ON THIN ICE
MERMAID COVE
(Mermaid Cove - Book 1)
RED TIDE
(Mermaid Cove - Book 2)
BREAKWATER
(Mermaid Cove - Book 3)
MAYHEM AND MISTLETOE
(Mermaid Cove - Book 4)
HIDEAWAY HALL
LOCKDOWN
IN CREPT EVIL
CAUGHT IN THE MIDDLE
(Seattle 911 – Book 1)
TWIST OF FATE
(Seattle 911 – Book 2)
HINDSIGHT
(Seattle 911 – Book 3)
DEAD SILENCE

JENNIFER HAYDEN

(Seattle 911 – Book 4)
IN PLAIN SIGHT
(Seattle 911 – Book 5)
DIRTY LITTLE SECRETS
(Seattle 911 – Book 6)
DANGEROUS LIES
(Seattle 911 – Book 7)
BLACKOUT
(Seattle 911 – Book 8)
UNFORGIVEN
(Seattle 911 – Book 9)
BACKFIRE
(Seattle 911 – Book 10)
HAUNTED
(Seattle 911 – Book 11)
JUST WHISPER
(Seattle 911 – Book 12)
THE RECKONING
SEE NO EVIL
(The Meadows – Book 1)
HEAR NO EVIL
(The Meadows – Book 2)
SPEAK NO EVIL
(The Meadows – Book 3)

WWW.JENNIFERHAYDENBOOKS.COM